"I'd love to try it sometime."

She saw it, in her imagination. Her finger, dipped into the glass jar of luminous, pale golden Corzo honey. Lifting it to his lips. The swirling pull of his mouth against her fingertip. Hot, tender suction. The flirtatious twist of his tongue, licking away every drop.

"Ah, yeah," she said, distracted. "I'll...get you some. To taste."

"Love to." His deep, resonant voice was caressing her senses like a brush of fur.

"But why?" she demanded. "I appreciate the interest, but if I decline partnership with MossTech, why interest yourself in Corzo?"

"I need a favor from you."

Tension was building inside her. "I'd be happy to help any way I can, but what could I possibly do for Marcus Moss, the CTO of MossTech?"

He looked her right in the eyes. "I need for you to marry me."

* * *

How to Marry a Bad Boy
by Shannon McKenna is part of the four-part
Dynasties: Tech Tycoons series.

Don't miss a single one!

Their Marriage Bargain
The Marriage Mandate
How to Marry a Bad Boy
Married by Midnight

Dear Reader,

I recently encountered a new word which delights me: sapiosexual, a person who is turned on by intelligence. (Raising hand.) But not only intelligence, of course. Rock-hard muscles, a sense of humor and a heart of gold definitely don't hurt. But I'm having such fun with my Tech Tycoons, with scientist, research analyst, mathematician and engineer heroes and heroines.

In Book Three, bad boy extraordinaire Marcus Moss, CTO of MossTech, has never committed to any woman for more than a weekend. Now it's his turn to face his controlling grandma's marriage mandate. Striking a cold, hard bargain with someone seems the best way to proceed. Brilliant geneticist Eve Seaton seems perfect. He helps get funding for her genetics start-up, and she pretends to be his bride. Easy-peasy, right?

Wrong. Because Eve takes his breath away. Now they've gotten more than they ever bargained for...

I hope you like this third installment of the Dynasties: Tech Tycoons series, *How to Marry a Bad Boy*! Don't miss Book One, *Their Marriage Bargain* (Caleb and Tilda's story), and Book Two, *The Marriage Mandate* (Maddie and Jack's story). And coming soon, Book Four, *Married by Midnight* (Ronnie and Wes's story)!

Follow me to stay up to date! Look for contact links on my website, shannonmckenna.com.

Happy reading!

Warmest wishes,

Shannon McKenna

SHANNON McKENNA

—

HOW TO MARRY A BAD BOY

HARLEQUIN®

DESIRE™

ISBN-13: 978-1-335-58140-2

How to Marry a Bad Boy

Copyright © 2022 by Shannon McKenna

Harlequin Enterprises ULC
22 Adelaide St. West, 41st Floor
Toronto, Ontario M5H 4E3, Canada
www.Harlequin.com

Printed in U.S.A.

Shannon McKenna is the *New York Times* and *USA TODAY* bestselling author of over thirty romance novels, ranging from romantic suspense to contemporary romance and even to paranormal. She loves abandoning herself to the magic of a story. Writing her own stories is a dream come true.

She loves to hear from readers. Visit her website, shannonmckenna.com. Find her on Facebook at Facebook.com/authorshannonmckenna, or join her newsletter at shannonmckenna.com/connect.php and look for your welcome gift!

Books by Shannon McKenna

Dynasties: Tech Tycoons

Their Marriage Bargain
The Marriage Mandate
How to Marry a Bad Boy

Men of Maddox Hill

His Perfect Fake Engagement
Corner Office Secrets
Tall, Dark and Off Limits

Visit her Author Profile page at Harlequin.com, or shannonmckenna.com, for more titles.

You can also find Shannon McKenna on Facebook, along with other Harlequin Desire authors, at Facebook.com/harlequindesireauthors!

One

"You're pranking me, right?" Marcus Moss demanded. "Tell me it's a prank."

Gisela Velez, his office manager, clucked her tongue. "Any woman on my list could easily play your temporary wife. Please. Consider it."

"What do I have to do to make you all understand?" he roared. "I will not play this game! I refuse! Get it through your heads!"

"You're not the only one in the game, Marcus," his sister-in-law, Tilda, reminded him. "A lot of careers are on the line."

Marcus Moss, chief technical officer of MossTech, shot to his feet with a murmured obscenity, shoving his chair back from the huge, cluttered desk.

Afternoon light filled his big corner office. He glared

around at his sister, Maddie, Tilda and Gisela, all of whom were breaking his balls today. Ruthlessly.

Gisela had been with him since he began working at MossTech, before he made CTO. She was knowledgeable and competent, and managed his Seattle office with an iron hand when he was out of the country dealing with the far-flung MossTech satellite labs. He had great respect and affection for her, usually. But not today.

Gisela folded her arms over her large bosom, frowning as if he were the unreasonable one. "We're not asking you to fall in love on command. We're asking you to cut a deal."

"You don't have much time before the ax falls," Maddie said. "Your thirty-fifth birthday is in seven weeks, and if you're still unmarried, controlling shares go to Uncle Jerome, and MossTech is screwed."

Marcus closed his eyes, cursing under his breath. The specter of his great-uncle Jerome Moss getting a controlling interest in MossTech was the price of noncompliance with his grandmother's ill-conceived marriage mandate. Even after retirement, Jerome still itched for executive power over MossTech. He'd wanted it ever since he and his brother, Marcus's grandpa Bertram, had founded the company. It had been an uneasy power struggle for the past fifty years of the company's existence, and Gran was using that fact now, ruthlessly. At the risk of hurting herself and MossTech, a company she co-owned, and where she had been chief executive officer for decades. Getting them married, at all costs, meant that much to her.

But it was a nightmare for her three grandchildren. Or rather, just for him, at this point. Caleb had gotten lucky last year. Maddie, only a few weeks ago. They were home free, by the grace of God. Good for them.

"So?" Maddie prompted. "Earth to Marcus. Pick up the pace, buddy."

"What do you think I'm doing?" he protested. "I'm trying to protect as much of our work as possible before Jerome trashes everything we've built over the last several years since we took over. Stop distracting me!"

"Our suggestion buys you time," Tilda urged. "Make a mutually beneficial arrangement with someone from Gisela's list. You don't have to pretend it's a real marriage. Gran knows better than to complain at this point."

"Like it's so easy," he retorted. "But I'm not like Caleb, Til. I've made it clear to everyone I ever hooked up with that I'm not interested in long-term commitment. I don't want the real thing. And I *certainly* don't want a fake thing."

Tilda's green eyes narrowed. "Come on, Marcus. Women drop at your feet like overripe fruit. You snap your fingers, and they jump."

"For a hot weekend fling, sure! That's *not* what's on the table!"

"You're sulking because the burden of Gran's marriage mandate has fallen on you now, right?" Maddie said. "You hoped Caleb and I would crash and burn before you, and you'd be off the hook. But no. Amazingly, it worked out for us."

"That's great, and I'm glad for you, but you shouldn't have indulged Gran like that. Now she thinks she's solved your lives. That it's my turn for her magic touch."

Tilda and Maddie exchanged guilty smiles. "I wasn't calculating Gran's wishes when I fell in love with Jack, Marcus," Maddie said. "I was suiting myself."

"Same here, with me and Caleb," Tilda added.

"Yeah, and so will I," Marcus snapped. "I won't comply. You knew I wouldn't, Caleb knew it, and Gran should have known it, too."

"She's trying to compensate for past mistakes," Tilda said. "She thinks she's helping you, in her clumsy, bossy way. She's really not trying to punish you."

"She's been trying to manage me since I was a toddler," Marcus said. "She could never do it then, so what makes her think that I'd behave now?"

"Do you remember that video call you made from that rice paddy in Indonesia?" Maddie asked. "The screaming argument heard round the world?"

"The one where Gran tried to pick out my date for your wedding? Oh, yes. I remember that conversation all too well."

"You said that you'd pick someone randomly out of a hat before you'd go with one of her choices," Tilda said. "And guess what? It gave us an idea."

"I was joking, Til," he said through his teeth.

"Yeah, well, we're not. Draw a name, Marcus. See who comes up. C'mon. It'll be fun."

"I started with the MossTech personnel and narrowed it down to women who've been hired for temporary special projects," Gisela told him. "They're smart and ambitious. They have already signed NDAs for the company, and we can write a specific contract for this. They aren't permanent MossTech employees, and we're making the limits clear. They can also refuse without any harm to their jobs. I even checked it out with HR. I wrote an algorithm to sort out eligible single women of a certain age, and I asked around to make sure they weren't engaged or living with their boyfriends. It's the best networking opportunity that they will ever get. It's weird for everybody, I admit, but desperate times call for desperate measures, right? And who wouldn't want to be the MossTech Hottie Dreamboat's temporary wife?"

"That's Caleb's title, not mine," Marcus growled.

"Nope," Tilda informed him. "You inherited the title when Caleb married me. Now poor Caleb is just a regular harried family man, frantically juggling family and career. Earn the name, Wonder Boy."

The smiles she was exchanging with Maddie and Gisela set his teeth on edge. "Do not yank my chain," he warned them.

"Lighten up, bro," Maddie soothed. "I know from experience how hard it is to power-shop for a spouse with brutal time constraints. Caleb only had a month to find someone last year when Gran came up with this mandate. We're trying to give you a jumping-off point."

"Yeah, right off a cliff!"

"Speaking of cliffs, if Jerome takes over, he'll do serious damage to the terms of the merger with my dad's company, which will hurt Riley Biotech's employees," Tilda said. "Help me out here, Marcus. Please. It's not just about you anymore."

"Talk to Gran," he said through his teeth. "I didn't create this mess."

"Buy us time," she pleaded. "Eight hundred people in Riley Biotech are counting on me to protect their livelihoods. Make an effort. Keep Jerome guessing. You have an escape route, remember? The marriage won't be forever. I'll show you the contract Caleb and I used. Use it as a guide. Tweak it however you like."

"No. I won't turn cartwheels for Gran. It's humiliating."

"So's getting your ass fired," Gisela said sourly.

"Come on, Marcus," Maddie coaxed. "You never intended to marry anyway, right? It's not like you're giving up anything real."

"My pride, my dignity, my integrity?"

Gisela rolled her eyes. "Pah. My cousins set me up with Hector at Uncle Luiz's wedding, and we were engaged two days later. It's been thirty years, and it worked. Aside from his snoring, anyhow. How is this any different?"

"At least you can be sure that any person contracted to do a special project for MossTech has been vetted for smarts," Maddie encouraged.

"Did Gran demand a DNA swab? Inspect their teeth? Request their medical records?"

"I didn't speak to Mrs. Moss about this at all. And they're all nice, respectable young women, so be polite." Gisela's gaze challenged him as she pulled a spreadsheet from a file and plucked an empty gift bag made of brocade-textured midnight blue paper out of her purse. "I don't have a hat, but we can use the bag from the Dior J'adore perfume you gave me on my birthday. I simply love the stuff, by the way."

"Glad to hear it," Marcus said grimly. "It wasn't enough to keep you on my side, though, was it? What do I have to give you, Gisela? Emeralds? My own heart's blood?"

"It's in all of our best interests to stave off the apocalypse," Gisela lectured. "You know that Jerome will fire your administrative staff the minute he fires you, right? We've been sending out résumés for weeks. The stress is very bad for morale."

Marcus had not, in fact, thought of that. He was appalled. "No way!" he said blankly. "Why would he do that? He'd be shooting himself in the foot to fire you!"

"Jerome's never been known for his good sense," Maddie observed.

"You know this place inside out," Marcus said to Gisela. "Our operations, our engineers, our history, the labs worldwide. Jerome would be insane to cut you loose!"

"He'll never trust me," Gisela said, her voice resigned. "I'll be out the door the day he fires you. And I'd really hoped to get all the way to retirement with this job. I don't want to roll the dice again at my age. So you're not the only one with skin in the game, okay? Sebastian!" she bawled through the door. "Bring me some scissors!"

A young assistant scurried in with a pair of scissors clutched in his hand, eyes wide and curious behind his glasses.

Gisela handed him the spreadsheet. "Chop those up, drop them into the gift bag."

Sebastian scanned the list as he snipped names. "Is this for the bride drawing?"

Marcus winced. "The whole admin staff knows about this circus?"

"That's none of your business, Sebastian," Gisela said sternly. She gave Marcus a guilty glance. "I had to ask around for the candidates' relationship status, so word got around. I was as discreet as I could be, but…"

"Right," Marcus growled. "I get it."

Sebastian waved a scrap of paper. "Nix Barb Jennings," he advised. "She met a guy at a conference in Vegas. Now she's got stars in her eyes and can't stop giggling."

"Thanks for the tip." Gisela twitched the scrap from him and tossed it in the trash.

Sebastian stuffed the strips of paper into the bag and placed it on the desk in front of Marcus, his eyes bright with anticipation.

"Out you go, Sebastian," Gisela said briskly. "Chop, chop."

Sebastian slunk out, crestfallen.

"You're telling me, with a straight face, to pick a name out of this bag, walk up to some random woman I don't even know, and ask her to marry me," Marcus said.

The women all spoke in unison. "Yes."

"Bro," Maddie said. "If anyone in the world can, it's you. Not to be crass, but you're rich, you're smart and you're smoking hot. Whatever this woman's professional aspirations are, you can sweeten the pot. She'll say yes. Unless she's in love with someone already, in which case, no harm, no foul. Just draw again."

"You enjoy the thrill of uncertainty, right?" Tilda said. "Aren't you the guy who loves extreme sports? This will break the spell. Get you moving in the right direction."

"Yeah. To another continent, maybe."

Gisela sniffed. "I've always gone over and above for you, Marcus. You owe me this. Just try before you kamikaze all of our careers, okay?"

"Do not guilt-trip me," he snarled. "I'm not the one piloting the death plane!"

Gisela held out the gift bag. "That changes nothing for the rest of us. And I'm not afraid to piss off my boss, since I'm about to be fired anyhow. Pick a name."

Screw it. He was outmaneuvered, and they all knew it. He shoved his hand into the bag, rummaged around... and around.

"Stop stalling," Maddie said.

"Stop nagging," he retorted, yanking out a strip of paper.

"Who is it?" the three women all demanded, all at once.

He gazed at it, frowning. "Eve Seaton," he told them. "Never heard of her."

Tilda let out a gasp. "Oh! I know that name! Caleb was talking about her. Everyone wanted her, but she'd only accept a short-term contract. Caleb would mortgage the farm to get her on his team, though. He's still hoping that she changes her mind."

"What's her specialty?"

"Genetics." Gisela sat before his computer, typing with blinding speed. "She's brilliant, they say. They hired her to lead a team that's genome sequencing some kind of fast-growing root-rot fungus. Let me...yes. Dr. Eve Seaton. Here. Take a look."

Marcus circled behind Gisela and leaned to look at the personnel photo on the screen. The shot had been snapped for her lanyard. She was brunette, and her dark, wavy hair was scraped back severely into something, a bun, a braid, a ponytail, who knew. The observer was given no clues about the rear details from that squarely frontal pose, just a faint fuzz of curling wisps around her forehead. She wore harsh, black-framed glasses, a white lab coat that blended in with the white background in the overexposed shot so that her hands and face seemed to float in an otherworldly sea of white.

He leaned closer. Her eyes pulled him, in spite of the glasses that somehow did not obscure them at all. Big, deep-set, a bright, light-catching gray. Full of calm challenge.

He leaned closer and inhaled a choking whiff of Gisela's J'adore. He teased what oxygen he could out of the air and tried not to cough.

Eve Seaton's other features were too washed out to make much of them, but she looked serious, prim. She had a heart-shaped face, delicate points to her jaw. Her lips were pressed tight, so it was hard to tell their true shape. In this picture, her eyes dominated.

After a moment, he realized that the women were exchanging smug looks.

"I bet this one's as smart as you, bro, if not smarter." Maddie had that little-sister nyah-nyah taunting tone. "Maybe you should draw again."

"Don't jerk me around," he growled. "I outgrew that garbage in kindergarten."

Their smothered giggles put him over the top. He was done with this interchange.

"Ladies, it's been real," he said curtly. "Talk to you later."

"Wait!" Gisela clicked with the mouse. "She's in the genetics lab on the fourth level of the Rosen Building, and her office number is 450. Take this." She rummaged through files and held one out. "This is everything I could collect on her. Educational bona fides, CV, professional organizations, scientific articles. You can make her dreams come true…in exchange for this insignificant favor that costs her nothing. Hmm?"

Marcus took the file. There was no way to remove those women from his office other than throwing them out bodily, so he left himself, striding through the cubicles outside. Their occupants looked away quickly as he passed, sensing his volcanic seething.

Unfortunately, the hapless Sebastian hadn't gotten the memo. He jumped up from his desk. "Hey, Mr. Moss! So how did it go? Who'd you pick?"

Marcus jabbed his finger in Sebastian's direction so savagely the kid jerked back, though he was ten feet away. "Not. Another. Word."

Sebastian recoiled, blinking rapidly. "Um, ah, yeah. Sorry. Sorry."

Marcus strode on, ashamed at himself for snarling at a bumbling dweeb like Sebastian. He headed straight for the door to the courtyard in search of air, sky.

It's not just about you anymore.

You're not the only one with skin in the game.

Just try before you kamikaze all of our careers, okay?

Goddamn Gran for dumping this mess on him. If he had only himself to consider, he'd walk away from MossTech without a care. Even if it had been his brother Caleb's career on the line, he'd have cut loose. He was confident that Caleb would thrive. His brother was doing great. Wildly in love with Tilda and his newly discovered little daughter, Annika, high on the euphoria of getting his best friend Jack Daly back from exile. Jack's name had been cleared of all wrongdoing, thanks to Maddie, who was Jack's new true love.

And all the love and devotion around here was putting him in a sugar coma.

But the thought of Gisela and the rest getting fired…

damn. And there were Tilda's people from Riley Bio-tech as well, all of them hanging on his conscience. It would be a bloodbath.

Marcus stopped in the center of the garden courtyard at the enormous fountain. Water ran smoothly over a huge, gleaming black granite globe.

Marcus opened the file. It was full of articles from scientific journals, co-written by a group of research-ers. Eve Seaton's name always led the list.

He was caught by a photo of Eve Seaton on a stage a few years ago, receiving an Oskoff Prize for excellence in biotechnology. Smiling, surrounded by beaming colleagues, holding a crystal plaque. She wore an embroidered charcoal gray silk gown with a high Chinese collar. It fit her body like a glove. Nice body.

The prize had been for the genetics in a project called Corzo. He scanned the documents. She and her team had engineered a fast-growing perennial grass that never needed to be aerated, and was genetically tweaked to sequester huge amounts of carbon from the atmosphere. After two years, a field planted with Corzo could suck more carbon from the atmosphere than a similar-sized plot of primeval rain forest, while also producing a very protein-rich seed that could be eaten by humans and livestock alike. Endangered honeybees also thrived on its flowers. Nice touch. Corzo multi-tasked like a boss.

The articles Gisela had gathered touted Corzo as being not only edible, but tasty. There was one about how Eve Seaton and her team had partnered with local bakers to develop Corzo recipes. A local magazine touted the Corzo Holiday Tasting Basket with an article entitled "Merry Christmas! Toothsome Treats for a Hopeful Future."

There were photos of her and her team in the article, next to a huge table with an array of baked goods, baskets of pasta, cakes, cookies, pastries. One picture showed Eve dipping a Corzo cracker into a cheesy dip. In another, she wore a little black dress and bright lipstick, laughing as she lifted a piece of what looked like a cinnamon roll.

Lovely smile. Pretty, soft, full lips. Nice figure. Tall, willowy. Stacked.

He pulled out his phone, hit Gisela's contact. She answered. "Boss?"

"Does Eve Seaton's Corzo project have funding?" he asked.

"It did, but it fell through last year for some reason," Gisela said promptly. "Great project, huh? You could get Caleb behind that in no time. He'll want her on board for the Greenroofs urban planning projects he's doing with Maddox Hill Architecture."

"Yeah, right. Bye, Gisela."

The other phone in his other jacket pocket rang, and he cursed under his breath. He should have left it in the drawer where it wouldn't bother him. It was the phone he kept for his sex life, which was rigorously separate from his work phone. Lately, with all the gossip about his need for a wife, he was being hounded by everyone he'd ever slept with.

The display read Teresa Haber. A weekend fling from several months ago. Not someone he particularly wanted to talk to again.

Might as well nip it in the bud right now. He put the phone to his ear. "Hi, Teresa."

"Hello, Marcus." Her voice was low and seductive. "I heard some shocking gossip about your grandmother forcing you to find a bride. Is it true?"

"Yes, but it's covered," he assured her. "Have a good evening, Teresa."

"Oh, so you found someone? Who did you—"

He closed the call. None of her damn business.

He looked at the article in the file, at Eve Seaton's laughing face. On the other side of the fountain was the Rosen Building, and in that the genetics lab. Office 450.

At this hour, the courtyard was nearly empty. People with families were hurrying home to their personal lives. Eve Seaton had probably left the building. Maybe she was out getting a drink with girlfriends, colleagues, who knew. But his feet carried him inside, to the central elevator bank. He got inside, hit the button for the fourth floor.

The elevator opened, and several people got onto the elevator he'd vacated. He strolled through nearly empty halls until he saw Office 450. Locked.

He continued on to the lab Gisela had specified. Inside, a tall Asian guy was emerging from clean room airlock.

Marcus approached him. "Excuse me. Is Eve Seaton still here?"

"Yeah, in the clean room." He pointed at a lone, heavily swathed figure at the far end of the clean room, visible through layers of protective glass beyond the airlock.

"Thanks." Marcus walked over to the window.

Eve Seaton's back was to him. She was slim, she had regal posture, and that was all he could tell about her, dressed in all that protective gear. She could have been an astronaut, with the gloves, the booties, the hood, the goggles, the mask.

Which made it harder to justify to himself. He was staring at a person swathed in a coverall, peering into a microscope. A person who had no idea he was there.

As spectacles went, it was as interesting as watching paint dry, yet here he stood, contemplating his possible future wife.

Not bored at all.

Two

Eve stowed her gear in the bin to have it freshly sterilized, and rolled her stiff shoulders, exhausted. She should have gone home hours ago. Cooked a healthy dinner with vegetables in it. Done some yoga. But no, instead she was clocking in ridiculous hours on the MossTech genome sequencing project. All in a vain attempt to keep herself too busy to dwell on that bastard Walter. If not for him, she wouldn't have needed this job at all. She'd be doing her own start-up, bringing Corzo to a world that badly needed it.

It had been months, and she still could barely believe it. Walter had been so supportive, so admiring of her mission. He was an accountant by profession, a natural money-man, and that was what she needed to shore up Corzo, and compensate for her weak points. Right?

Yeah, he was a money-man, and no mistake. She

just hadn't understood quite what kind. Not until he stole her inheritance, plus every last penny she'd saved over the past several years, and ran off, with his side piece in tow.

Stop it. If she started thinking about how far Walter had set her back, she got into a toxic feedback loop and got so angry, she felt sick.

A glass of wine and a sandwich would help. Some sleep would not suck, either. She saw herself reflected in the glass, and winced. The synthetic hood plastered her hair down, made her scalp damp and her glasses fog. She should go back to contacts, but they made her eyes itch. Besides, Walter had preferred the contacts. He found her sexier without glasses.

Ha. Screw sexy. Screw Walter. She pushed the glasses up on her nose and twisted her hair into a careless bun as she emerged from the airlock.

"Excuse me."

The low, quiet voice behind her made her spin around with a gasp, heart pounding.

"Sorry if I startled you," the owner of the voice said. "Are you Dr. Eve Seaton?"

Eve tried to form words, but the vocal mechanism wouldn't engage.

Marcus Moss. In the flesh. He was the secret reason she'd chosen a job at MossTech, over other equally prestigious options. A dizzy, girlish part of her brain had hoped she might run into him sometime. Like a fawning groupie.

He took a step forward. "I didn't mean to startle you. I should have introduced myself. I'm Marcus Moss."

Oh, but she knew. CTO of MossTech, brilliant engineer and master of all that he surveyed, who played a starring role in her dreams. The X-rated ones, anyway.

Hoo, boy. He was so fine at close range, it verged on the indecent.

Moss waited for a response, a polite frown of puzzlement between his dark, well-shaped brows. He was biracial, and she'd heard that his father was Japanese, or maybe Korean. And damn was he attractive.

His sensual mouth quirked in a small smile. He was used to this. Speechless, open-mouthed girls who forgot their mother tongue when he smiled at them.

"Sorry I scared you," he said gently. "I promise, I'm not dangerous."

She almost laughed. *The hell you're not, buddy.*

"I'm MossTech's chief—"

"Chief technical officer, yes. I'm aware of that." Thank God, her voice functioned again. "Sorry, my voice got stuck for a second."

"So you know who I am."

"Of course. Everyone knows who you are." *But they don't have feverish, erotic dreams about you. They don't set Google Alerts for any scrap of news about you.*

If she let herself think about how weird that was, she'd scare herself, so she'd decided that her crush was a private, harmless coping mechanism. Like collecting saltshakers, bird-watching, tai chi.

"You're working on the fungus genome sequencing, correct?" he asked.

"That's right." She aimed for a professional tone, but it came out breathy and high-pitched. "So, Mr. Moss? What can I do for you?"

"I'm not sure yet," he said. "But I have… I guess you could call it a business proposition to put to you."

Eve brushed a wisp of hair off her forehead. "Business? Me? What kind?"

Marcus Moss opened his mouth and then closed it again. He looked almost nervous. "Could we go someplace to talk?" he asked. "I need a drink. And some dinner. Have you eaten?"

"Ah…well…" She glanced at the leggings and tee she wore under the coverall. "I'm not dressed for going out."

"We'll go someplace quiet. I'm not dressed formally, either."

Ha. The hell he wasn't. His impeccable designer clothes looked amazing. Fresh, crisp, perfectly cut, loose where they needed to be loose, deliciously snug where they needed to be snug.

That body would look amazing in any clothing. Or none at all, if it came to that.

Eve pushed that distracting thought away before it could mess her up.

"So?" he prompted, after she'd stared blankly for too many seconds. "Dinner? Steak, seafood, Asian, fusion, sushi, Mexican, Turkish, Vietnamese?"

"Um…okay," she said faintly.

"Which one? Got a preference?"

"After twelve hours in here, I'm incapable of making decisions," she said. "Anything's fine. You're the executive. Making decisions is your job description, right?"

His dark eyes narrowed. "Yes, but I try not to throw my weight around."

"That's thoughtful, but tonight, you'd be doing me a huge favor if you took this burden from me, because I am fried. Excuse me, while I grab my purse."

She hurried off before she could do any more nervous

babbling. Dinner with Marcus Moss, after twelve hours of genome sequencing? She looked like a wet rag. Why couldn't she be one of those women who were always put together? Their makeup stayed put, their clothes didn't crease, their hair stayed smooth. Her mother had been one of those, for all the good it did her. Mom had always looked perfect, even if the sky was falling. Which it frequently had, for her.

Hanging in the closet of her office was a burgundy merino dress she'd left there one day when it proved to be too hot. Shape-wise, it was the equivalent of wearing a flour sack, but at least she didn't look like she'd just come out of the gym. She ran a brush through her hair, debating between hair loose or messy bun.

Messy bun won the day. A neat bun would be better, but at this hour, with low blood sugar and shaky hands, a neat bun wasn't going to happen.

She pawed through cluttered drawers until she found a patterned silk scarf. She knotted it around her neck and fished mascara and some eyeliner out of the depths of her purse. She hadn't worn makeup in months. The Walter debacle had put a damper on her urge to decorate herself. See what happened when she risked love and romance? She handpicked another parasitical user, just like her father, and the others. She'd be better off focusing on her mission.

But this was Marcus-freaking-Moss, damn it, and she was putting on mascara.

Sadly, she had nothing to cover the purplish shadows under her eyes, nor was there lipstick in her purse's miscellany. She bit her lips, to get some color. Slicked on lip balm.

Marcus Moss was waiting outside her office when

she came out. Something inside her chest went ka-thunk. Beautiful things happened to that man's face when he smiled.

"So?" she asked. "Where to?"

"There's a steakhouse near here. Do you know Driscoll's?"

"I haven't been there, but steak sounds great."

The cool September evening was rather drizzly and damp. They must have talked about something on the short walk through the streets of downtown Seattle to the restaurant, but when the maître d' ushered them to a table, she had no memory of what they'd said.

They knew him here and treated him like royalty. The place was hushed, low murmurs mingled with soft clinks of cutlery. She was dazzled by the spectacle of Marcus Moss, tasting wine. The splash, the sensual swish, then he held it to the light to admire the color, then he sniffed the aromas, eyes closed…and then, oh, God…he sipped it.

She practically orgasmed on the spot.

Marcus nodded his approval to the server, who poured out wine, laid out their menus and vanished.

"So," she said. "It's a steakhouse, so I guess it's silly to ask what's good here."

"After a twelve-hour day, I suggest the entrecote, the salad of fresh greens topped with char-grilled fresh artichokes, olive oil and Amalfi lemon, and a side of herbed potatoes," he said.

"God, yes." She pushed the menu away. "Go no further."

"Not even to the desserts? They're very good."

She tasted the red wine, which was deep and aromatic. "One thing at a time," she told him. "First, tell me why I'm here. I'm burning with curiosity."

His gaze slid away from her face. "It must seem strange, for me to bother a complete stranger at work after a long day."

"Actually, we have met before," she said.

His eyebrows rose. "We have? When? Where?"

Oh, crap. She regretted putting him on the spot. "The first time was five years ago. I saw you and your brother at the World Agri-Tech Innovation Summit. I also saw your talk at the Prescott Institute. And I was at the Future Innovation trade show last year. My team planned to rent a booth, but my funding fell through, so I just came as a spectator."

She'd also come to admire Marcus himself, but he didn't need to know that. Better go easy on the wine, or she'd blurt out things that would make him uncomfortable.

"I'm sorry I didn't recognize you," he said.

"I was one out of a huge crowd of fans," she assured him. "Your project was amazing. I was rooting for you, though the Bloom Brothers' project was also spectacular. I'd love to collaborate with those two. I've been working on a project for a few years that I think would interest them, a grain that's engineered to sequester carbon. I have various strains for different climates and growing seasons."

"Corzo, yes," he said. "I'm familiar with it."

Her jaw dropped. "You are?"

"Of course," he said. "It's an impressive project. You'd be a good fit with the Blooms. You have a holistic mindset similar to theirs. I could organize a meeting. I'm very good friends with their publicist."

Eve was startled. "Really? That would be amazing."

"Sure," he said. "So what happened before the trade show? Why didn't you get a booth and take part in the contest? Did you have a setback in your research?"

Eve choked on her wine, dabbing her mouth. "Not in the research, no."

"Sorry," he said swiftly. "None of my business."

"It's okay," she told him. "It's common knowledge, after all. I have no secrets."

"Okay. So…?" He waited.

Eve set aside her wineglass and organized her thoughts. "I was engaged last year," she admitted. "To my financial manager. People told me at the time that wasn't the greatest idea, but I pooh-poohed them. The first of my many mistakes."

He winced. "I think I know where this is going."

"Yeah, everyone saw it coming but me. Walter was part of the firm that had managed my mother's estate, upon her death. What was left of it, anyway."

"Left of it?"

"She was the heiress to the Travis retail fortune, before she married my father," she explained. "He cleaned her out. Stripped everything he could before he left for good. All that was left was the real estate he hadn't been able to liquidate. After my mother died, I intended to sell that property, and use the cash to launch my start-up."

Marcus waited patiently, his eyes intent on her face.

"I'd gotten involved with Walter in the meantime," she went on finally. "He was an account manager at my mother's investment firm, though I didn't know that when we started dating. He'd researched my assets, extensively. And then he asked me out."

"I see," he murmured.

"My team and I were planning our start-up," she said. "Walter offered to lend us his skills. It seemed perfect. But as soon as the property sales were finalized, and the money deposited in my account, Walter disappeared. With all my money."

He hissed through his teeth. "What an asshole."

"Yeah," she agreed. "To make it sting even more, his twenty-four-year-old female administrative assistant disappeared along with him. The fair Arielle."

"Have the police made any progress in finding him?"

"Not yet," she said. "He's smart. Methodical. Ironically, that's one of the things I found really attractive about him. He must have been planning this before he even met me."

"Slime," Marcus said forcefully.

"Yes," she said. "Romantically, I'm over him. Nothing could be more unsexy than a bloodsucking thief. But the money, oh, that hurt. It wasn't a vast sum, but it would have gotten us going."

"Us?" he asked. "Going where?"

"Me and my Corzo team," she explained. "That was our seed money. Money management is not my strong suit, so Walter's promise to help us was very seductive to me. I'd fantasized being free to geek out on the science, and leave the bean counting to him. I should have known it was too good to be true."

"Luckily for you, Walter is shortsighted," Marcus said. "Corzo has incredible commercial potential. I confidently predict that Walter and Arielle will watch your stock prices skyrocket, and see you start making nine figures right around the time their stolen loot runs out, and they have to downgrade from their luxury hotel to cheaper lodging. Where they will start arguing about money. What should they pawn first? His motorcycle, or her emeralds?"

She laughed out loud. "What a great image. Thanks for that. So, that happened not long before I had to send the money for the booth at Future Innovation. We'd been selected as finalists, but my life fell apart, so I withdrew the project and came as a spectator. Trying not to feel sorry for myself."

"You're entitled to feel angry," he said. "I hope they nail that asshole and his girlfriend both. They can rot in jail and ponder their character flaws."

"Me, too. But even if I got that satisfaction, I'll never get the money back," she said. "They're eating it, or driving it, or snorting it up their nose as we speak."

"Even so, this is a blip in your screen," he said. "You'll get past it."

"I intend to," she told him. "That's why I took this job. We're all working at other places until we scare up seed money again."

"Is that why you'd only agree to a temporary contract here at MossTech?"

Eve was startled. "For a CTO of a company as enormous as MossTech, you certainly know a lot about the terms of my very recent employment."

Marcus shrugged. "Us executives. We know things. It's our job."

She laughed. "Well, yes, that's why. We need a stroke of luck. Even with all of us saving, we'll need outside investors. My mycologist, Sara, arranged a meeting with some investors from Hong Kong last week, but they made me nervous."

"What are their names? I know a lot of the players."

After a split second, Eve decided there was no reason not to tell him. "The Yueh Xiang Group."

He shook his head. "I know the Yueh Xiang," he said. "Shady as hell. They'll eat you alive and spit out your bones."

Her heart sank. "Well, hell. Maybe I'm developing a nose for sleaze. Too late to sniff out Walter, but better late than never."

"Definitely. Which brings me to the reason you're here."

At last, his mysterious agenda. She was so dazzled she'd almost stopped wondering why he'd asked her out. "I'm all ears."

"I was impressed by Corzo. Have you considered partnering with MossTech?"

"We've considered every option," she said. "But my team and I want to maintain control of the patent."

"I could help you find investors independent of MossTech," he said. "The idea sells itself. I mean, feeding the honeybees? Get out of here."

She laughed. "I know, right? Corzo honey is delicious. It has an exotic flowery aroma like no other."

"I'd love to try it sometime," he said.

She saw it in her imagination. Her finger dipping into the glass jar of luminous, pale Corzo honey. Lifting it to his lips. The swirling pull of his lips against her fingertip. The flirtatious twist of his tongue, licking away every drop.

She pulled herself back to reality. "Ah, yeah," she said, distracted. "I'll…get you some. To taste. It's great in tea. Or, um…yogurt."

"Love to." His deep, resonant voice was caressing her senses like a brush of fur.

"But why?" she demanded. "I appreciate the interest, but if I decline partnership with MossTech, why interest yourself in Corzo?"

He took a sip of wine. "I need a favor from you."

Tension built inside her. "I'd be happy to help any way I can, but what could I possibly do for Marcus Moss, the CTO of MossTech?"

He looked her right in the eyes. "I need for you to marry me," he said.

Three

Ouch. Not smooth. But there was no good way to slip a zinger like that into a dinner conversation. It was like throwing a lit firecracker on the table.

Eve Seaton gazed at him, her pink mouth slightly open. A puzzled crease between her elegant dark eyebrows. Waiting for the punch line of the joke. Because it had to be a joke, right?

She sucked her lower lip between her teeth, then let it go. It gleamed, soft and pink, in the candlelight. "Excuse me?" she asked faintly. "I'm not following."

"Just temporarily, of course," he said hastily.

Eve shook her head. "I don't understand," she said. "I don't even know you."

"I'm sorry. This is very awkward," he said. "I'm proposing a business arrangement. For complicated legal reasons, I need to be married before I turn thirty-five, or suffer consequences I'm not willing to accept. There isn't anyone that I want to marry, nor have I ever wanted marriage in the first place. One solution to this dilemma could be to approach someone who has a project I could support, and in return, she'd consent to being my wife for a limited period. To solve my problem."

He paused for a moment. She just stared. The silence was absolute.

"In name only," he added carefully. "Of course."

"Ah…yes." Eve lifted her glass of wine and took a gulp. "Of course."

As she set it down, he noticed her well-shaped, unpainted nails. Her slender fingers. Her hand was trembling.

That alarmed him. "I didn't mean to scare you. I wouldn't ask something like this of just anyone. It had to be someone for whom I could return the favor in some concrete way. I picked you out because I thought I could help you with your project wholeheartedly, and wouldn't find doing so a burden. But if this upsets you, forget I said it."

"You didn't scare me," she said. "You surprised the living hell out of me."

He let out a relieved breath. "Do you know about this marriage requirement? The way people gossip, I figured you might."

"When I'm in work mode, I don't think of anything but work," she said. "Besides, I'm new here. I don't really know people well enough to participate in gossip."

Huh. That was refreshing, after all the whispering, giggling, sidewise looks and the exhausting tsunami of ex-lovers and flames like Teresa, some still unmarried, others freshly divorced, filling his voice mail with seductive come-ons.

Eve wasn't like that. She had a mission, and she was committed to it. Her priorities were out there in blazing neon, for all the world to see.

"How did you get into this fix?" She sounded fascinated. "It sounds so antique."

"It is," he agreed. "My grandmother decided that my brother and sister and I are too driven and work-focused, even though she was the one who drove us to be that way. She was the previous MossTech CEO, and she was the one who wanted us to take over management of the company, about eight years ago. In her mind, she raised us and she warped us, so now it's her sacred duty to fix us. Like knocking the dings out of a dented car, and her strategies are about that subtle. Blunt force."

"Oh, dear," she murmured.

"My brother and I have to be married by age thirty-five, and my sister by age thirty."

"Or else…what?"

"Or she gives controlling shares of MossTech to my great-uncle Jerome. He's wanted to be the big boss from the beginning, but my grandparents always kept him in check. At least, up until now."

Her wince showed that Uncle Jerome's reputation as a grade-A asshole had spread far and wide. "That seems a rather extreme punishment."

He let out a short laugh. "Oh, ya think?"

"But I thought your brother was married," she said. "With a daughter, even."

"Yes, but it's recent. Caleb got lucky. He hooked up with an ex that he was still in love with. Turned out that she'd had his child years before. Gran frothed with joy.

In fact, this whole mess started because Gran got wind of Tilda's kid being Caleb's. It flipped a switch inside her. She really wanted her great-grandchild. And not just Annika. She wants more. A whole dynasty of them. So here we are."

"Wow," she said. "Drama to the utmost."

"Oh, always," he said. "We Mosses excel at drama. My sister, Maddie, did okay, too. She's getting married to Jack, who she's crazy about, in ten days, on the eve of her thirtieth birthday. She's timing the ceremony to sign the paperwork at eleven fifty-nine."

Eve laughed. "Just to mess with everyone's head?"

"Yeah, she and Jack think it's hilarious," he said grimly. "Ha. Ha. Ha."

"But the joke's on you, right?"

"Exactly. They can afford to laugh. If MossTech goes to the dogs, it won't be their fault. There are a lot of jobs at stake, not just mine and Caleb's. Jerome would clean the place out of everyone loyal to us."

"That's awful," she said.

"Yes," he said. "I hate being jerked around. But I hate hurting all those people more. And handing Moss-Tech to that bastard while he cackles and rubs his icy hands together, God, that stings. Caleb and I worked hard to build this company up. Not to brag, but we brought MossTech into the third millennium. All that work, for nothing."

"I see," she murmured.

"Anyway, that's what's driving this bizarre proposal," he concluded. "Gran's paperwork stipulates that I stay married for five years. We can of course keep our own private living spaces, and conduct our private lives however we like, as long as we're discreet and put on a good show on public occasions. That's all I need from you. In return, I'll do everything in my power to help Corzo launch and thrive."

"Um...wow."

The server arrived with their meals. They fell silent as plates of food were arrayed before them. Steaks sizzled on their platters, but Eve didn't pick up her fork. She looked pale.

"If it makes you uncomfortable, forget it," he urged. "I didn't mean to offend you."

"I'm not offended," she said quickly. "On the contrary."

"Try your steak," he urged her. "I should have waited until you'd eaten before springing this on you."

He started into his own food, but he couldn't relax and enjoy it until he saw her take a few dainty bites. Her reaction worried him. She'd been so sparkling before, quick to laugh, readily telling him all about herself, and his offer had quenched all that. Now she looked colorless, subdued. He missed how she'd been before.

He refilled her wineglass. "I think I've made a mistake," he ventured in the strained silence. "I wish I could take it back. I want you to enjoy your meal."

"I'm sorry if I give that impression," she said. "But my last attempt at matrimony made me swear off the institution for life. So I don't know what to say."

"You're like me," he said. "I never wanted it, either, and not wanting it makes you a uniquely perfect candidate. You won't be sacrificing anything important to you, so you have nothing to lose and everything to gain."

"You make a strong case for it," she said. "You don't

think your grandmother would sense that the marriage was fake?"

"I don't care if she does or not. I don't think she'll give us a hard time. At this point, she'll be grateful if she can save face without destroying the company that she helped my grandfather found."

"Am I the first person you've asked?"

"Yes," he said. "The situation is embarrassing, but I wouldn't mind getting behind something like Corzo. The world needs it. My brother and I wanted Moss-Tech to be all about service to the world. Uncle Jerome doesn't share our philosophy."

She laid aside her fork and knife, steepling her slender hands together. "Just to be clear. If I were to agree, how would it play out?"

His spirits shot up. "It would have to be soon," he said. "We'd meet with my lawyers. Bring your own lawyer, and I will foot the cost for whatever you're billed for having the contract reviewed. If the terms are acceptable, we apply for a marriage license and get married as soon as possible. I want to present my new bride at my sister's wedding. Surprise, suckers."

She snorted with laughter. "Sounds fun. When's that wedding, again?"

"Ten days. We have to move fast. Jerome will be there, so there will be drama."

"What kind of drama?"

"He's a foul-tempered asshole," Marcus said. "He'll be aggressive and rude and inappropriate. He was to Tilda and to Jack. You are, of course, free to tell him where he can stick it, which Tilda and Jack both did. Are you conflict-averse?"

"I don't actively seek it out, but I don't let people walk over my face, either. Walter was a special case."

"Screw Walter. This is a great way to get back everything he took from you and more."

Their conversation paused as a server came to take their plates. Eve leaned forward. "Do you need an answer right away, or can I take some time to think about it?"

Marcus realized he should have thought this through. "Not too much time," he said. "The time I have to put this deal together is running out, so if you decline, I have to move fast to find someone else. Could you give me an answer by tomorrow?"

"Seems fair," she said.

"I'll put my number into your phone. Call me if you have questions."

Eve passed her smartphone to him. He entered his name and number into her contacts and returned it. "There," he said. "Done."

The server reappeared behind them. "Can I tempt you with any of today's dessert specials?" he asked. "We have a fruit trifle with crème Chantilly, a blackberry millefoglie tart with vanilla cinnamon ice cream and chocolate lava cake."

"Sounds delicious, but not tonight," Eve said. "Could you call me a car? I usually grab a bus to get home."

"Of course." The server turned to Marcus. "And for you, sir?"

"No dessert." He turned to Eve. "I can call a Moss-Tech car to take you home."

"I'm fine with a car service," she assured him.

He could well imagine that she wasn't ready to give her home address to a strange man. Particularly one making offers as strange as his. "Use Egret Cars," he told the server.

"Don't you need one, too?" Eve asked.

"I'll walk," he told her. "My apartment isn't far from here."

"Must be nice, to live so close to work," she said.

"I'm out of the country a lot. When I'm in town, I don't like to waste any of my time commuting. So I bought a place that's minutes away by foot."

"That's great," she said. "I love this city, and I do have a car, but the traffic exhausts me."

The server appeared again. "Miss, your car is here."

Eve stopped by the cash register, but Marcus waved her onward. They stepped out into the chilly breeze and stopped next to the idling Egret sedan.

"Did we walk out of there without paying?" she asked him.

He shook his head. "I have an account. I'm not a bad cook, but after a long day, I'm too tired to deal with it, and this place is right on my way home."

"I get you," she said, with feeling. She pulled her jacket close against the wind, her bright silk scarf fluttering. "Thank you for a very…unique evening."

"You're welcome," he said. "I try to keep things interesting."

"Well, then." Eve looked flustered. "I'll let you know my decision soon."

He held out his hand, and she took it—*whoa*.

Sensations flashed through him, like wind lifting his hair except it was everywhere. A caressing, whole-body rush of startled awareness. He was hyper-conscious of every detail of her. The curl of her lashes, the sweep of her brow, the curiosity in her bright eyes.

Her lips looked like they would be so soft to kiss.

She pulled her hand away and got into the car. He shut the door after her, maintaining eye contact until the car pulled away, and her eyes were lost to sight.

Dial it down, Moss. This wasn't about emotion. That was the point of picking out a random stranger for this. No feelings. Simple. Controlled. Detached.

But his eyes followed the red taillights until they turned. A deep, tingling hum pervaded his whole body. Eve Seaton made him feel intrigued, challenged, tempted. Aroused, just by a brief timid handshake.

He couldn't help but wonder what effect a kiss might have.

Four

Marry Marcus Moss? What in the actual *hell*?

Eve wanted to bounce and shriek, but the driver was a grizzled older man who looked tired. He did not need any overwrought silliness inflicted on him, so she held it in, but she was still rocking back and forth, her hands over her mouth. She still caught some nervous looks from the guy in the rearview.

Omigod. Marcus Moss's number, in her phone. She half expected the device to burst into flames. He was brilliant, gorgeous. She'd actually had a good time. Laughing, talking, drinking, nerve endings caressed by his resonant voice, his aftershave tickling her nose. A more distilled kind of fun than she'd ever had.

And after all the sensory overload, he'd proposed. Holy…freaking…*cow*.

It was a marriage proposal, turned inside out. She'd

been chosen specifically because he didn't love her, want her or envision her in his future. That made her perfect, for his purposes. Her lack of desirability made her desirable.

Oof. Put that way, it stung a little.

Not that she blamed him. He'd never seen her before. The only problem was her Godzilla-sized crush on him, which would disqualify her, if he knew about it, emotional intensity being precisely what he did not want. The driver reached Sara's apartment. She leaned forward, hand in her wallet. "What do I owe you?"

"It's paid for, ma'am," was his laconic reply.

"But...but I told him he didn't need to—"

"Done deal," the guy said.

"At least let me give you your tip," she said. "How much was the—"

"Tipped already, twenty-five percent. Don't sweat it, ma'am. The gentleman took care of it."

Did he, now? After she'd specifically told him not to. She murmured her thanks and made her way up the two flights of stairs on the outside of the house to the top-floor apartment where Sara lived. She texted with her phone instead of knocking.

Sara! Please be awake.

Sara didn't take long to respond. What are you doing up at this hour?

I'm outside your door, she texted.

?? her friend replied.

A light flipped on a minute later, and Sara's slim shadow moved behind it. She twitched the curtain aside to peer out onto the porch.

She pulled the door open. "What the hell, Eve? Is something wrong?"

"I have news," she said, as she entered her friend's apartment.

Her best friend, Sara Cho, was a brilliant mycologist. They had met at CalTech and done postgraduate work together. Sara was her dream colleague. Smart, creative, a sense of humor, rock-solid principles.

Sara, too, currently worked at another lab, at Ballard ChemZyne. She was recently and bitterly divorced, not long before Walter had made his escape. She and Eve had already been friends, but the wretched perfidy of men was a great bonding agent.

Sara beckoned her into the kitchen. Her long black hair was twisted into a thick glossy braid. "So?" she prompted. "What happened? Are you okay?"

"I… I don't know," Eve said. "I think I'm about to do a really crazy thing."

"Really? Fun crazy, or scary crazy?"

"I'm not sure, but I'm scared right now," she admitted.

Sara flipped on the lights and studied Eve's face. "Spill it, girlfriend."

"Marcus Moss asked me to marry him," she blurted.

Sara's face went blank. "Hang on. Marcus Moss, celebrated billionaire CTO of MossTech?"

"Yes," she squeaked.

"The gorgeous studmuffin you've had a sloppy crush on ever since you shared an elevator with him at the Agri-Tech Summit five years ago?"

"The very one," she said.

"But you've never even been introduced to him!

Though I know you only went to MossTech because you were hoping to scope him from afar."

"Wrong! I went there because it was the best job offer!"

Sara rolled her eyes. "Sure it was. I didn't blame you, after Walter. You deserved to indulge in some eye candy. But marriage, Eve? How in the hell?"

"A temporary marriage," she explained. "A fake marriage. Sorry, I should have led with that. His grandma insists he get married before his thirty-fifth birthday or else he and his brother, the CEO, lose control of Moss-Tech to their great-uncle. Jerome Moss."

Sara made a face. "Ouch. That won't go well."

"Exactly. So that's it, Sara. I'm the lucky girl. He never wanted to marry, so he's picking out a stranger that he doesn't give a damn about, who will expect nothing from him. A marriage in name only." She paused. "So, uh. It's not like I have to have sex with him, or anything."

There was a brief silence. Sara let out a burst of smothered laughter. "*Have* to have sex? Get real. It's me, Sara. Say, 'get to have sex,' and I'll buy it."

Eve snorted. "If you must. It's not like I 'get' to have sex with him. Happy now?"

"Not quite," Sara said. "Because if you're not getting hot, sweaty, pounding sex with Marcus Moss out of it, what the hell *are* you getting out of it?"

"Corzo," Eve said.

Sara's jaw dropped. "No way!"

"For real," she said. "He'll help us launch Corzo if I do this for him. Favor for favor. If I stay legally married to him for five years, he'll help us find more investors, et cetera. He thinks Corzo has loads of potential."

Sara pressed her hands to her mouth. "Eve. Oh my God."

"I know, right?"

Sara grabbed her shoulders. "So? Have you said yes?"

"I have until tomorrow night to decide," she said.

"So what's stopping you?" Sara asked. "What's the catch?"

Eve bit her lip. "You know the catch," she said, in a small voice. "It's my dumb crush on him. I get all flustered and red in the face, and I talk too much, and you know he's going to notice, sooner or later. It's exactly what he's going to these insane lengths to avoid. And when he does notice, I'll feel so stupid and small. I'm just not sure if I can survive feeling that small again. It might break me."

"Oh, honey." Sara pulled her into a hug. "I bet the spell will break as soon as you get close enough to smell his pits."

"I was close enough tonight," Eve said, her voice muffled against Sara's hair.

"Yes? And?" her friend prompted.

"He smelled delicious," she admitted. "I could have eaten him up with a spoon."

"Yikes," Sara murmured. "You, my dear, are a sad case."

"Oh, I know," she agreed.

Sara hugged her again. "I'll tell you what. There are a couple of different ways this can go. Option one, you play it cool. Stay distant, fulfill your side of the bargain like the professional you are. Take what he has to offer and squeeze him like an orange."

She laughed soggily. "Okay. And option two?"

"In option two, you take this opportunity to seduce the hell out of him, get him to fall in love with you… and squeeze him like an orange."

That cracked them both up.

"Me, seducing him," Eve muttered. "As if."

Sara looked disapproving. "Why the hell not? You've got the looks. You're just too busy and distracted to exploit them. You've got the brains. You're highly motivated. You'll have the opportunity. The guy will be your husband, for God's sake. It's doable."

"Sara, I love you, but you're a very bad influence," Eve said.

"I know," Sara agreed. "And I'm very excited about what Marcus Moss's help could mean for Corzo. But truthfully? I love you, babe. You've already been through a lot of shit, and your happiness is more important to me. Only do this if you can do it without hurting yourself. Maybe even have some fun with it. Otherwise, we'll muddle on as we have so far."

Eve gave her a misty, tearful smile. "I'm going to do it."

Sara jumped up. "Omigod! Omigod! For real?"

"Yeah." Eve pulled out her phone and found the contact. She glanced at the kitchen clock. It was past 1:00 a.m., but it was his fault she was awake so late. She hit Call.

He answered quickly. "Hello?"

"Mr. Moss? This is Eve Seaton."

"Eve." There was a smile in his voice. "Call me Marcus. Have you come to a decision?"

"Yes, I have," she said. "I'll do it."

"Excellent. I'm so glad. Can you meet me tomorrow

afternoon, at my lawyer's office? The legal department at MossTech is in the Kobe Tower, eighth floor."

"I can find it," she said.

"Great. I'll text you the exact time when I talk to their office tomorrow."

"I'll be there. Thanks for this opportunity. My team will be thrilled."

"I'm the one who should thank you. You've just saved MossTech's ass."

"We'll thank each other," she said. "Good night."

She looked at the phone in disbelief. "We draw up the contract tomorrow," she said to Sara.

They grabbed each other, dancing with joy.

Sara pulled open the fridge and took out a bottle of champagne. "I was saving this for my birthday, but if this doesn't call for a toast, I don't know what does. Get out the champagne flutes."

Pop, the cork yielded, hitting the ceiling and bouncing off the table and to the floor. Pale foam fizzed sensually from the bottle. Sara poured the cold, pale wine into the delicate champagne flutes Eve had set out on the table and handed her one.

"To the success of all of our endeavors." Eve lifted her glass.

They drank, and Sara promptly refilled them to the brim.

"To squeezing the sex god like an orange," Sara said. "No matter what comes out."

They exploded into giggles, clinked glasses and drank.

"I can't believe I'm doing this," Eve said as Sara filled her glass a third time.

"You'll crush it," Sara said firmly.

Eve set her glass on the table and wiped away an embarrassing rush of tears. "Sorry," she quavered. "I'm a little bit drunk."

"On two glasses of champagne?"

"And the wine I drank with Marcus," she explained.

"That has a nice ring to it," Sara encouraged. "'The wine I drank with Marcus.' I like the sound of it."

"So do I!" Eve wailed. "But it would be so stupid to get all intense about him—"

"Babe," her friend said wryly. "You already are intense about him."

"I know. And if I did as you said, and tried to seduce him, I'd melt like ice cream all over him and make a big sticky mess."

It took a while for her to stop shaking. Sara handed Eve a napkin to dab her eyes, and blow her nose.

"Interesting," Sara said thoughtfully. "You never showed this emotional intensity about Walter. Even when he robbed you blind and slithered off into the tall grass with Arielle."

"Oh, come on, Sara," Eve muttered. "I don't even know the guy."

"Well, babe," Sara said philosophically. "For good or for ill, you're gonna know him now."

Five

Marcus was glad that he'd worn the black Versace suit when he saw Eve enter the room at the Seattle Municipal Court. She looked good. He was glad he'd requested this room, too. True, this was a business arrangement, but why conduct important business in an unattractive setting?

Hence, the corner room, with floor-to-ceiling windows. Too bad they couldn't have used the roof terrace, but it was drizzling. Besides, he had to be careful not to overdo it.

Eve looked amazing. She was wearing a knee-length fitted burgundy dress of some textured fabric that hugged every dip and curve. Hair twisted into an elegant French roll. Sexy black pumps. Her heavy, black-framed glasses looked like a bold and fearless fashion choice in the context of that outfit. Or maybe that was just the way she held herself. Chin high, eyes meeting his, proud and regal. Elegant.

Her silver-gray eyes silently said, *let's do this*.

His cousin, Ronnie, stood next to him, blue eyes full of curiosity. She was his great-uncle Jerome's daughter, but she was five years younger than him, and she'd been raised with Marcus and his siblings for much of her childhood. She was as close to him as a sister.

He'd asked Ronnie to be his witness because he couldn't bear either Caleb or Maddie in that role right now. They were floating on cloud nine, with the condescending vibe of two lucky bastards who'd been kissed by fate. They'd found rapturous happiness and fulfilled their familial obligations, in one blow.

Woo-hoo. Yay for them, but it stuck in his craw.

Ronnie had dressed up for the occasion in a minidress of black-and-white-checked wool, black tights, black pumps and glittering jet earrings, her red hair in a high braided bun. When he and Eve had met with the lawyers, they'd agreed to keep it simple and private. The officiant, and one witness apiece. No one else needed to know until Maddie's wedding. Just Ronnie herself, who was sworn to secrecy.

Eve had brought a friend for her own witness, a small, beautiful Asian American woman who looked him over with bold interest.

Marcus stepped forward, taking Eve's hand. "You look beautiful," he told her.

"Thank you. I wasn't sure how much I should dress up, but I figured, a woman doesn't get married every day of the week."

"You look perfect." He turned to her friend. "How do you do? I'm Marcus Moss."

"Sara Cho," the friend said. "I'm glad to meet you."

"Sara is a member of the Corzo team," Eve said. "She's our mycologist."

"Then I'm sure we'll be seeing a lot of each other," he said to Sara, smiling.

Marcus gestured at Ronnie, who came forward. "This is my cousin, Ronnie Moss."

Eve shook Ronnie's hand. "I didn't know Marcus had close relatives, besides his brothers and sisters."

"None but me," Ronnie told her. "My dad was their grandpa Bertram's little brother. If it hadn't been for them and my aunt Elaine, I wouldn't have made it through my childhood intact at all." She rolled her eyes. "Insofar as any of us can be considered intact. I'm Jerome Moss's daughter. How intact could I be?"

Eve gave him a startled look, but Ronnie caught it and spoke up. "Don't worry," she assured Eve. "I'm on Marcus's side."

"Ah… I didn't mean to imply—"

"And it's completely my dad's fault that we're talking about sides at all," Ronnie went on. "Dad has an ego the size of Texas. I genuinely wish that Aunt Elaine's marriage mandate included me, too. I'm turning thirty in a few months. There's nothing I'd like better than to get married at the eleventh hour, like Maddie's doing, and throw it right in Dad's face. He deserves it."

"Sounds unnecessarily risky," Eve said carefully.

"Not for me. I'm already engaged." She held out a spectacularly large diamond ring. "I'm a sure thing. It would be a moral slap to my father. We're not on very good terms. If you haven't noticed." She looked embarrassed. "Sorry. Didn't mean to lay my family crap on you."

"That's okay," Eve assured her. "I haven't spoken to my own father in over six years."

Ronnie looked impressed. "You've got me beat."

"Yes, I always perform well in screwed-up-family one-upmanship competitions," Eve told her. "I score very high."

"Then you'll fit right in," Ronnie said warmly.

The officiant walked in, a stern-looking gray-haired man with a no-nonsense air. The officiant began the ceremony.

As the man spoke, something strange happened to Marcus. All sound retreated, as if his mind had floated free of his body. All he could hear was his heart, thudding, panicked, deafeningly loud. Marcus focused on Eve's face. She was his anchor. She kept him from floating off to God knew where.

Fortunately, Eve was watching the officiant, and didn't appear to notice his condition. Her beautiful red lips were moving. Then the officiant's lips, too. He heard nothing. Oh, crap, now the guy was looking at him. He needed to respond, but to what, he had no clue. He struggled to tune in. To breathe.

"...to marry Eve Elizabeth Seaton?" The officiant's voice sounded very far away.

They looked at him expectantly. Ronnie, standing behind him, was frowning. She snapped her fingers.

Pay attention, she mouthed.

"Uh... I do," he forced out.

The officiant frowned. "No. We haven't gotten to

the vows yet," he said sternly. "I said, are you, Marcus James Moss, free to lawfully marry Eve Elizabeth Seaton? The affirmative response is, 'I am.' Is that quite clear?"

"I am," he said grimly.

Evidently Eve had already declared her lawful freedom, because the guy moved briskly on.

And he was back to the real world. His normal self. Thank God. What the *hell* had happened? Was that a panic attack? This was a fine time to start having them.

He could follow along now, well enough to recite the appropriate vows. He could hear Eve's clear, musical voice quietly echoing them. He hoped whatever the hell that was wouldn't happen to him again. It was like being taken over. Extremely unsettling.

The time came for rings, which he'd picked out the week before. He pulled out two thick bands of white gold, rounded, glowing bright. Eve had gotten her short nails manicured. They gleamed with a transparent, pink-tinted glossy sheen. The ring looked good on her. The skin of her hand was velvet soft. Holding it was like having a bird resting in his hand.

"…pronounce you man and wife. You may now kiss the bride." The officiant sounded like he was doing Marcus a big favor.

Marcus met Eve's startled eyes and leaned down to brush his lips against hers.

Or at least, that was the plan. A dry little peck to seal the bargain. But as soon as her soft lips touched his, he was jarred by a feeling he'd never experienced.

The world just…opened up. In a flash, he saw everything, felt everything, sensed everything. There were no barriers between him and her mysterious allure. He sensed the endless possibilities of that kiss with startled wonder.

He leaned into her softness, the tender sweetness of her lips. Eve's hands splayed on his shirtfront, but she didn't shove him away. Her nails dug in, seeking a better grip as her mouth opened beneath his—

A nervous cough, and Marcus froze, remembering where he was. *Whoa.*

He retreated from the embrace. Eve did the same. His face felt hot. The officiant had a save-it-for-the-wedding-night scowl.

Ronnie pressed her lips together. She looked like she was trying not to smile. Sara Cho looked shocked.

"Excuse me," he said softly.

Eve's eyes fell. "It's okay," she whispered.

He was appalled. Control was his thing. He kept his sex life compartmentalized. It never touched work, family, MossTech. But this bargain with Eve was wound up inextricably with all of those things. Sex with Eve would be a disaster in terms of control.

In every other way, the idea yanked him like a tow chain.

"Sorry," he said again, helplessly.

"You already apologized," Eve murmured. "You do that out of sheer habit, right? I won't take it seriously if you don't. But we should avoid tongue-kissing, as a rule. We didn't cover that kind of thing in the contract."

She was smiling, teasing, giving him an out. He tried to match her energy. "Uh, yeah. Absolutely."

They signed the paperwork and thanked the judge, who promised to register the certificate at the appropriate office. The four of them walked outside onto the wide sidewalk outside the building. It was late afternoon, and the misty drizzle of early fall in Seattle had formed a fuzz of tiny droplets on the fibers of Eve's burgundy wool coat.

He was a married man. Eve looked dazed. Ronnie's speculative gaze shuttled back and forth between them. Sara Cho's face was cold. Hostility radiated off her. Eve's best friend thought he was an opportunistic slut. Not a great beginning.

"Could I invite all of you out to dinner?" he asked. "We should celebrate."

"That sounds great," Eve said.

"Sorry, I can't," Sara said, her voice clipped. "I have another engagement."

"I can't either, sorry," Ronnie said. "I promised to meet Jareth, my fiancé, at the airport. He's in from LA for the weekend. But I really do look forward to getting to know you."

"So do I," Eve said warmly.

"Say hi to Jareth for me," Marcus said, out of politeness, though he'd never particularly liked the guy. He seemed the perfect fiancé on the surface, smooth and well-spoken and ambitious, always with a big smile and a hearty, friendly manner, but Marcus had the nagging sense that there was nothing much underneath the pleasant veneer.

But whatever made Ronnie happy was fine with him.

"Would you excuse us for a moment?" Sara's voice rang out. "I need to speak to Eve in private." She grabbed her friend's arm and dragged her out of earshot.

"Uh-oh," Ronnie murmured. "Eve's best girlfriend

hates your guts. And I would, too, after that shocking performance. Good God, Marcus. Control yourself."

His cousin's intent gaze made him uncomfortable. "Don't go looking for drama where there isn't any."

"Don't go pretending it doesn't exist when it's glaring right into your face," Ronnie said. "That kiss, dude? What in the actual hell?"

"Don't make it into a thing, Ron—"

"I'm not the one who made it into a thing," Ronnie told him. "You did that yourself, and it's irresponsible. Confusing, for her. This will blow up in your face if you don't watch it."

"I'm starting to regret asking you here. I should've brought Gisela."

"You think Gisela wouldn't have ripped you a new one if she'd seen what I saw? Gisela has more at stake than I do if you screw this up. Think about Gisela and all the rest of them, and keep that bad boy zipped up tight, okay? I say this because I love you."

"Are you done with the sermon?" he asked, through gritted teeth.

"For now, if you're good. But there's plenty more where that came from."

"Don't you have to run the airport? You don't want to keep Jareth waiting."

"Be good." Her voice was soft but forceful. "Congratulations. I hope this whole thing shakes out well for us all. But watch yourself. Bye."

She took off, calling and waving her goodbyes to Eve and Sara as she passed.

Marcus watched her disappear, still smarting from her reproof.

She was right. He had to keep things cool. He might have known that this would get complicated, full of hidden pitfalls. The classic hallmark of Gran's influence on his life.

Still, he couldn't blame Gran for the kiss. That was his own personal bad judgment. He had to own it.

Bad judgment or no, that kiss was going to haunt his dreams.

Six

"Sara, what on earth?" Eve was startled by the force with which her friend dragged her into the shelter of the courthouse portico. "What's gotten into you?"

"Where does he get off?" Sara hissed. "How *dare* he?"

"How dare he what?" Eve grabbed her friend's hand. "Because he kissed me?"

Sara huffed furiously. "Duh! Does he think you're just his for the taking?"

"Calm down," she soothed. "I think he just did that out of habit. He said he was sorry. Twice. No big deal."

"Oh! Will he nail you, too, out of habit? The first time you happen to be anywhere near a horizontal surface, boom, you'll find yourself with your legs in the air! Oops! Will he apologize then, too? I do not want you to be a notch on his belt, Eve!"

"I won't be," she assured him. "He's a perfect gentleman."

"Ha!" Sara snapped. "Not!"

"I'm bewildered. Aren't you the woman who told me to go for it? To squeeze him like an orange? Now you're all agitated just because he kissed me after being invited to do so by a municipal judge?"

"He didn't just kiss you, Eve!" Sara protested. "He was…sucking face!"

That jerked a startled laugh out of her. "Um, no."

"This is not funny," Sara said. "I know that I said to seduce him. But there is a huge difference between you seducing him, and him seducing you. Vast."

"Is there? I don't see it. It doesn't matter, because I don't intend—"

"It's a power thing, Eve. Don't you see? You're way more vulnerable than he is. I should never have advised you to do this! I was dazzled by the opportunity to get Corzo going again, and now I feel like a bad, selfish friend."

"Oh, no, no, no." Eve seized her friend and hugged her. "You're a great friend. You're panicking over nothing. This is a business arrangement, and we both stand to gain from it. He knows better, I know better. Trust me. We're grown-ups."

Sara snorted. "That's not what I saw."

Ronnie Moss passed by them, smiling and waving. They both waved back.

Sara's eyes brimmed with tears. "Please, be careful, okay?" she pleaded. "Keep that guy at arm's length. Promise me."

"Don't stress about me," Eve urged. "I'll be fine.

Put all that energy into figuring out how to start Corzo again. Tell everyone, so we can start planning."

"Okay," Sara said, her voice garbled with tears. "Okay, I'm on it."

Eve hugged her, and they walked back to where Marcus stood waiting. The cold wind flapped his long coat and ruffled his jet-black hair. God, he was tall.

"Congratulations," Sara said stiffly. "Enjoy your dinner. Eve, call me when you're back home, okay?"

"Of course," she said gently. "Talk to you later."

When Sara was lost to sight, Marcus crooked his arm, a courtly, old-fashioned gesture. She took his arm, and they fell immediately into step.

"Your friend is suspicious of me," he said.

"That kiss alarmed her," Eve explained. "She's afraid you'll sweep me off my feet. Give me unrealistic expectations. But it's okay. I'm chill."

"You're lucky to have such a protective friend," he said. "And she was right to disapprove. It was undisciplined on my part. It won't happen again."

Well, shoot. That was well and good, but his promise left her feeling rather deflated. "Already forgotten," she said crisply. "So? Where to?"

"It's early for dinner, but I thought we could find some place near here and get drinks. We haven't really done that part yet."

"What part of what?"

"The get-to-know-you chat over coffee or drinks that you do on a first date." He stopped, looking into a pub window. "This looks good. Beer, wine, cocktails. Shall we?"

She agreed and soon they were seated inside, listening to low-key blues music, studying a list of artisanal beers as long as her arm.

"Do you have decision-making capacity tonight?" he asked her.

"I just made one of the biggest decisions of my life, so by rights, I should be feeling depleted," she said. "But oddly enough, I know what I want. God forbid you should think that I'm a passive pushover."

"You're the farthest thing from passive that I've ever encountered."

"I'm not sure what that means, but thank you. I want a red wine like what we had at the steakhouse. It was warm and mellow and spicy, like a pine forest in mid-summer."

"That's a very clear and articulated decision," he told her. "My compliments."

"Yes, isn't it? I'm getting better at it."

The server passed their table. "We'll take a bottle of Salice Salentino," Marcus said. "Cantine Sant'Agata. Do you have a 2014?"

"I'll check." The woman gave them the menus and left, but not before casting a long, fascinated look at Marcus. It occurred to her that she was going to have to get used to that.

"So," he said. "Remind me how this goes. I don't do first dates very often."

"Really? I thought you got all kinds of action." She clapped her hands over her mouth. "Oh, God. That was rude."

He grinned. "Maybe, sometimes, but my encounters don't usually involve a lot of conversation."

"Ah." Her face reddened.

"So?" he prompted, after a mortified pause. "What do we talk about?"

"I don't date much, but we'd probably start with work," she began. "But we already know the basics. Then there's school, but I expect you and your lawyers went through my academic past with a fine-tooth comb, right?"

His eyebrows lifted. "Yes," he admitted. "But they only told me about the things that might be a problem."

"To be sure I wasn't harboring a dreadful secret?"

He shrugged. "Your life is blameless. Notable only by the fact that it's so productive. I've read some articles. The ones you published in *Nature Reviews Genetics* and *Genome Research*. Amazing work. No discernible bullshit in any of them."

"Thanks," she said, pleased. She'd never been with a person who understood what she did in her job. Walter had tried for a while, but he'd given up on the pretense very early on.

"What about you?" she asked. "I know you've been CTO for the last several years. That you and your brother took the reins of MossTech together."

"Yes, exactly. Before that, I was working as an engineer in Indonesia, setting up micropropagation labs for NGOs. Troubleshooting lab hardware and software."

"Do you speak Chinese?"

"Yes, and Tagalog, Malay and Javanese. But my Chinese is strongest. I spent a few years there, during college and after. I use Chinese all the time, but I never have the time to drill down and make it better, the way I'd like to."

"That's you being a perfectionist," she said.

"I guess you'd know."

They paused in their laughter as the server arrived with the wine. Eve was all ready to enjoy the sexy spectacle of wine tasting again, but as the server poured wine into the glass, Marcus gestured at her.

"Have her taste it," he said.

"Oh, no, you do it," she urged him.

"I want to watch you while you taste it." His deep voice was silky. "If you like the scent of a pine forest in the summer."

"Oh. Um. If you insist." She felt incredibly exposed for the brief ritual. She swirled, inhaled and then lifted the glass to her lips.

The complex flavor of the aromatic red wine expanded in her mouth. Deep, subtle aromas she'd never perceived before. Bitter herbs and sweet fruits, lavender, berries. Relentless drenching sunshine. She almost felt as if she were performing for him. Something intimate and sensual.

Oh, God, dial it down. It's just a sip of wine. She let out a sigh and signaled her approval. "It's lovely."

The woman poured, cast a final hungry glance at Marcus and left.

"Is it as good as the one we had at Driscoll's?"

"Better," she said. "The heavens opened up."

"I love it when they do that." He took a sip and sighed. "Ah, yes. Nice."

She was overheated. Sensory overload from every direction. And his deep voice stimulated all her tender, secret inner parts, setting everything aflutter.

She had to get this back on track. She'd promised Sara she'd stay cool.

"Okay, so we've covered employment background

and educational history," she said briskly. "We should move on to…how about family background?"

"What comes after family?"

"Oh, miscellany. Likes and dislikes. Hobbies. Music, books, sports teams, favorite TV series. If it goes well, maybe you might make it to politics, religion, hopes and dreams, worst fears, greatest heartbreaks, heart's desires."

"For you, the sequence is ass-backward," he said.

"How do you figure?" she asked. "We haven't even started."

"Certainly we have," he said. "Your hopes and dreams and heart's desires are all out there for the world to see. In blazing neon."

"How so?" She frowned, perplexed.

"You're that rare person who never wondered what her heart's desire is," he said. "You figured it out early on, and then you went for it."

"You mean Corzo?"

"Yes. I think I can guess what your worst nightmare is, too. A lot of us share that nightmare, and Corzo is an answer to it. A proactive, powerful, elegant answer."

"Thanks," she said. "That's very perceptive. But your professional efforts amount to the same thing, on a larger scale. A MossTech-sized scale."

"Scale doesn't matter."

Eve snorted. "Only someone in your position on that scale can afford to say a thing like that."

He studied her thoughtfully. "Maybe we should backtrack," he said, his voice neutral. "Go back to family. Hobbies."

She took a sip of wine, considering it. "Family's sure to hit a nerve."

"True thing," he agreed. "My family drives me out of my skull. And you're in the same boat, right? You told Ronnie you hadn't spoken to your father in years. You told me he ran through all of your late mother's money. Do I remember that right?"

"Yes. I lost Mom three years ago. Heart attack. I think it was years of pining, being hurt, hoping he'd change, always disappointed. It wore her heart out."

"I'm so sorry," he said. "Any other family?"

She shook her head. "I was an only child. By the time I was born, Mom knew better than to have more children with my dad, but she still couldn't bring herself to leave him. She was an only child herself. So sad to be all alone in the world and all that. My solitary state was definitely part of the opportunity that Walter smelled in the air."

The pulse of a classic old blues tune filled the silence between them.

"And your dad?" he asked.

Eve held out her hand. "Why, pray tell, are we starting with me?"

Marcus shrugged. "It fell out that way."

"Things don't just 'fall out' with you," she said. "You pilot them. You know in advance the results you want to obtain."

His brows drew together. "Is that a bad thing?"

"Depends," she said. "I want to know you, too. But I bet you prefer to know everything about everyone while remaining unknowable yourself."

His face was impassive. After a couple of minutes of silence, she started getting nervous. She had to suppress the urge to fill the silence with chatter.

"Is there something in particular that you want to

know?" he asked. "I'll tell you anything. Shall we go back to hobbies? I could tell you about my passion for extreme sports. Skydiving, parasailing, free climbing."

That measured voice made her toes tighten. She lifted her chin. "No. Just don't manage me. Don't evade or misdirect or flatter me. I'll call you out."

He nodded and poured wine into her glass. "I'll answer any question you want with total honesty, but you might as well finish. Tell me about your dad."

She sighed. "Well, it's like I told you. We're estranged. I don't see that changing. He was a bon vivant. He liked to party, he went on long, expensive vacations that lasted for months. He drank too much, he gambled, he liked drugs and the company of other women. My mother tried to divorce him, but every time, he persuaded her that he'd changed. He was very charming, and he cleaned her out. Once he'd liquefied everything he could, he left. That was six years ago."

"I'm so sorry," he said. "You're lucky to be rid of him."

"I don't know if I am rid of him," she said. "I keep meeting him. In a metaphorical sense, I mean."

"What does that mean?"

She instantly regretted blurting that out. It was the Marcus Moss effect. Ironic, since he was so good at holding things back. "I seem to keep meeting the same kind of man and having the same results, that's all."

"Elaborate," he said. "Now I'm curious."

"Oh, God, this is embarrassing. Can we let it go?"

He gave his head a shake and waited.

Aw, what the hell. "I first identified the pattern when I was an undergrad at CalTech," she said. "I'd moved in with Doug, my boyfriend, into his off-campus apartment. He kept telling me he'd cover the next month's rent if I'd spot him for this month. But the next month, it was the same story. That happened over and over. Soon I was paying groceries and utilities, too, plus cooking for him, doing his laundry and cleaning his cat's litter box. And this all while working in the lab, taking exams and writing my thesis on cell biology. After six months, a light bulb went on in my head. I packed my stuff and left."

"What an opportunistic prick," Marcus said slowly.

"Yes. Then there was my thesis adviser in grad school. We had an affair while I was working on a project under his supervision. I thought I was in love. How lucky to have a mentor so supportive of my research, right? Then he stole my work and published it as his own. He sent me a note, saying thanks for your contribution, couldn't have done it without you, et cetera. As if he could have done it at all."

Marcus's eyes narrowed in disgust. "Hack asshole."

"Yes, he was," she agreed. "That's how I pick 'em."

"What's his name?"

She was startled. "Why on earth do you want to know?"

"I want to make sure I never hire the bastard."

"Never mind," she murmured. "So, about a year ago, I decided, carefully, deliberately, to try again. And look at the card I pulled. Walter. There you have it. That's my reason for swearing off matrimony. I keep falling into the same trap. Walter seemed so different, you know? But then, so did Hugh, my thesis adviser. I should have known about Doug. He was just a good-looking zero, not much else to him. But all of them were opportunistic parasites. I've got a mysterious sign taped to my back that only guys like that can see. It says, 'Step right up. Help yourself.'"

Marcus was quiet for a moment, watching the candle flicker on the table between them. "I'm not a parasite, Eve."

She was horrified. "God, Marcus! I never meant to imply that you were!"

"You didn't. But it's important to state, for the record, that I will always give as good as I get, if not better."

"Yes," she said. "I'm sorry, I didn't mean to—"

"Don't apologize. If I sound like I'm angry, it's because I am. But not at you. I'm angry at Walter and Hugh and… What was his name? Dave?"

"Doug," she murmured.

"Doug. Your dad, too. I despise manipulative users. What a wasteful drain on your energy. I want you to blast off into orbit with Corzo, and shake them off forever."

She smiled at him. "What a lovely thought. I hope I pull it off."

"You will," he said. "I'll make sure of it."

They smiled as the server appeared with olives, little squares of hot rosemary focaccia and tiny knots of mozzarella. Once she'd retreated, Eve nibbled on a fat, savory red olive and gave him an encouraging nod. "Okay," she said. "Your turn."

"For what?"

"Family," she said. "So far, I know you have an interfering, manipulative grandma, a very difficult great-uncle with an ego the size of Texas. Then there's your cousin Ronnie, who is currently engaged, and a brother and sister, both happily paired. Right?"

"That about covers it," he said.

"What about your parents?" she asked. "Where are they in the mix?"

"Nowhere," he said. "My mother died when I was very small."

She was taken aback. "Oh, no. That must have been devastating."

He lifted his shoulders. "I don't know." His tone was distant. "I hadn't seen her for over a year when she died. My last memory was hearing her bitch about me on the phone to my grandmother. I was driving her crazy, evidently. She needed to get rid of me."

"Oh," she faltered. "Ouch."

"So she sent me off to Gran and Grandpa Bertram, where she'd already sent my brother, Caleb, and that was the last I ever saw of her. She never came to see us again. She died in a boat accident, not long after Maddie was born. I then proceeded to drive a series of nannies out of their minds. Gran tells me I was a hell-spawned monster. But to her credit, she never gave up on me. She hung in there, stubborn as a rock. We get that from her."

"You don't seem wild now," she said.

Marcus's gaze locked on to hers, and suddenly, a hypnotic glow of seduction was emanating from him. "Don't I?" he asked softly. "How would you know?"

She held out a quelling hand. "Do not even try to distract me. We're not done. You said I could ask you anything."

"Anything, yes, but not everything," he complained. "Enough, already."

"Anything," she repeated sternly. "How about your dad?"

He shook his head. "I cannot give you any satisfaction on that score," he said. "I know nothing about him."

"Nothing?"

"My mother lived in an expat enclave of beach houses

in Thailand, and she was partying hard, with a jet-set crowd. None of the three of us have a name or even a nationality for our fathers. All of that biographical data went down with the yacht."

"Oh," she murmured.

"The three of us got curious, and did genetic tests once, for fun," he went on. "Caleb's mystery half was mostly Spanish and Portuguese. Maddie's was mostly northern Africa. Mine was equal parts Japanese and Korean. No more leads beyond that, but I don't look like the pictures of my mother that hang in Gran's house, so I must look like some guy she rolled around with one night almost thirty-six years ago, and then never saw again. She was not a careful woman."

Eve was silenced by the bitterness in his voice. "I see why you evade the subject," she said. "Sorry I lectured you about it."

"I've never talked this much about my past to anyone."

"Then I'm honored," she told him.

The painful confessions had loosened them, somehow. They both finally relaxed into the conversation. They drank wine, ate finger food and worked their way through the more frivolous items on her impromptu first-date list. The appetizers were tasty, so they continued with entrees. A flaky vegetable pastry for her, a grilled lamb dish for him.

The time sped by. When a dessert cart rolled by, Eve shook her head. "I'm too full, and even if I wasn't, who could choose?"

"We can bring a sampler," the server offered swiftly. "You could try them all."

"Great idea," Marcus agreed. "Bring the sampler."

"And then I have to get home," she told him. "I need to call Sara, or she'll go into a tailspin, thinking that I'm...well. Never mind."

"Sacrificed upon the altar of my insatiable lust?" he suggested.

"Well, yeah," she admitted.

"I'll prove that my intentions are honorable. Oh, before I forget. I have an account at Federica Atelier. You'll need an evening gown for Maddie and Jack's wedding."

"Federica Atelier?" She was startled. "Marcus, get real!"

"She's a friend. She'll do it as a favor to me."

"But... But a Federica is one-of-a-kind wearable art! There's a waiting list six months long for a fitting with her! I have plenty of nice dresses, Marcus."

"This expense is on me," he said. "It's our first public outing as a couple, and I'm your husband now, remember? I can buy you a dress. It's not weird at all. Really. There was even a clause in the contract covering a clothing budget."

"But it's not necessary," she protested.

Dessert was laid before them, a tray with six little plates, each with a small serving of dessert, even a mini-ramekin of crème brûlée.

"A woman with great strain burdening her decision-making capacities should not be forced to choose between her pleasures." Marcus's voice had taken on that dangerously caressing tone that stroked something deep inside her, something that tingled and glowed. "She should taste them all."

"That's a very decadent mindset," she said.

"Decadent and luxurious, that's me," he said.

She gazed at him with narrowed eyes as the thought formed in her mind. "You let people think that," she said slowly. "You do it on purpose."

His eyes narrowed. "Meaning what?"

"It's a mask," she said. "You hide behind that persona."

"Many can bear witness to my decadence. It's heavily documented."

She let her spoon crack through the fine sugary glaze of the crème brûlée, and scooped up a bite. "Just because you play the part well doesn't mean it's not a part."

"I don't hide who I am," Marcus said. "Don't project fantasies onto me, Eve."

"I'm not," she told him. "I'm following my instincts."

He shook his head, his eyes cool again. "Maybe you're right. In any case, we should get you home. Sara will worry."

"Okay, but after two bottles of wine, we should both take a cab."

"I have a driver waiting," Marcus said. "He's outside."

"Since when? I never saw you call anyone."

He held out his watch, which had a digital touch-screen face. "If I push this, my phone texts a pickup request and my GPS location to my driver. I'll take you home."

"Oh, no. I'll call a car service, so you can—"

"We just got married. We're husband and wife, and we've never even seen each other's living spaces. Please?"

She threw out her hands. "There's no need."

"It would be my pleasure."

It was a reasonable offer. She'd been having a really good time with him. But the sexual awareness was a constant, rumbling hum in her mind. She had no idea what he would do if they were alone. Or, more to the point, what she would do.

If he started turning on his devastating, seductive charm, oh, Lord.

She was toast.

Seven

Marcus couldn't take his eyes off her. The rest of the world faded into the background. He wanted to know every detail. Her stories, her thoughts and opinions, and all the subtle, mysterious things about her that he had no names for yet. Being with Eve woke up new senses, new longings. New hungers.

He couldn't stop flirting. It was involuntary. He couldn't be any other way with her, unless he shut his damn mouth and sat there like a statue. With other women, he was good with seductive blather, but it was calculated, a means to an end. If he behaved in a certain way, he achieved a desired result. His technique had never failed him.

With Eve, there was no technique, just a sharp, clawing desire for something he couldn't even define.

Sex, of course. That was a given, but he wanted more than sex. Much more.

And he couldn't plan it or control it, or even describe it. He was hooked on her eyes, the tone of her voice, the curved lines at the corners of her mouth when she smiled.

Alvarez was waiting outside the restaurant in the black Porsche Cayenne SUV. Marcus opened Eve's door and without thinking, gave Alvarez her home address.

Then he looked at Eve's face, realizing how creepy that might seem.

"Is my street address one of those things you know because you're an executive?" she asked.

"No, I'm just a details nerd," he confessed. "I read your work file. I have a steel-trap mind for info like that. But I should have let you tell Alvarez your own address. That looked bad. Sorry."

"It's okay," she murmured. "A man probably shouldn't be blamed for knowing the street address of the woman he's married to."

"I appreciate your understanding," he said. "While I have you here in my clutches, can you schedule an appointment with Federica tomorrow? I think crimson would look amazing on you. I want you to make a splash."

"Alarming thought," she said.

"Why? You're gorgeous. I want to flaunt you."

She looked flustered. "Um. Fine. I'll, ah, arrange an appointment."

He was overdoing it. But damn… Eve, dressed in a sexy red evening gown that was exquisitely tailored to her pinup-girl body—how could any man not be openly enthusiastic about that prospect?

Damn, what were the odds, when he stuck his hand into Gisela's gift bag, that he'd pick out a stunner? Brilliant, too. Funny. Challenging. Intriguing.

But he felt like a clumsy adolescent. All this embarrassing intensity. He had to keep a lid on it, or it would blow up in his face, like Ronnie had warned.

"I'm sorry to drag you to hell and gone all over Seattle," Eve said.

"No trouble," he replied. "Kind of a long commute for work, though, isn't it?"

"Yes, it is. I got the apartment to be close to the first job I got in Seattle. The MossTech job is much more recent. I was going to get Corzo established, and then buy something out in the suburbs, with a big lawn where I could have a garden. But that fell through."

"Not for long," he said. "Things are changing for you."

The traffic wasn't bad, so they made good time. When the car pulled in front of her apartment building, they sat there silently for a moment.

"Would you, ah…like to come in?" she asked shyly. "You mentioned wanting to see my living space."

His heart rate spiked. "I'd like that very much."

Marcus followed her into the building, past the curious gaze of the doorman. She was on the eighth floor, and he could tell the second she unlocked the door of her apartment that the place was full of plants. He smelled flowers, the humidity, the rich scent of earth. Plants sweetened the air.

Then she turned on the light, and he almost laughed. The place was a jungle of hanging plants with long, dangling fronds, burgeoning and beautiful. Spider plants, hanging ferns, begonias, succulents. In front of the entire length of the picture window was a long, raised wooden box, bursting with a tall, luxurious grass.

"Is that Corzo?" he asked.

"It is. The latest iteration. I like to live with it day by day, so I can observe it."

He stroked a blade of grass with his fingertips. "It looks tough and enthusiastic."

"Oh yeah. It's the best," she said. "I'm fond of it. It's flexible, it's unfussy. It adapts to all environments. It's a champion of a plant. A really good sport. A farmer planting Corzo would have to go out of her way to screw it up."

"Great qualities," he said.

She looked abashed. "I love my plants. They're like friends, to me."

"I'd love to see a big planting of it."

"I can take you to some plantings nearby," she said.

"Great. It's a date." He wandered through her place and saw antique prints of botanical drawings decorating the walls. He leaned closer. "These are really beautiful."

"I have a thing for nineteenth-century lady botanists," she told him. "If I'd been born back then, that would have been me. Gardening, painting flowers, studying nature. If I'd been born into the ruling class, that is. Otherwise I'd have been hauling wood and dipping candles like all the rest. I'm so glad I was born in a time when I can be a scientist. And those lady botanists paved the way for me."

"Everyone should have the chance to develop their talents," he said. "We need all of our human capital to survive. The Moss Foundation supports educational programs all over the world. From early childhood education to college scholarships. We believe in it."

"I'm glad we're on the same page about something so important," she said.

"About this, too," he said, gesturing at her plants.

"You said you liked plants and gardening, back at the restaurant when we talked hobbies, but you're as nuts about it as I am. I breed flowers, too, in my greenhouse at home. It's the only thing that relaxes me."

"I'd love to see them," she said.

"You will," he promised.

"How do you take care of a greenhouse when you have to travel so much?"

"My assistants, Sven and Aram, come in to check on my babies while I'm gone. And I have an automated system. Watering, misting, humidity, plant food. Cameras, so I can monitor them remotely." He paused. "But I think they like it when I'm home. Probably I'm flattering myself."

She laughed. "I feel the same way. Let's go ahead and flatter ourselves. The plants don't mind our nonsense."

"Good thought," he said.

They smiled at each other. She was shorter now, having stepped out of her high-heeled shoes. She was padding around on her wool rug in her black-stockinged feet.

Her feet were very pretty. Small, narrow, arched.

"Would you like a glass of brandy?" she asked.

"That would be great." He followed her, through the living room and into the kitchen of the open-plan apartment.

Eve took two small brandy snifters from the cupboard, and pulled out a bottle of Camus. "It's been a while since I got this stuff out."

She poured out some brandy and passed it to him. Her hands brushed against his, and the brief contact reverberated through him like a rung bell.

He lifted his glass. "To our new partnership."

"To the fulfillment of our wildest dreams," she added.

"Amen to that." They clinked glasses and drank.

The brandy had a deep, mellow burn. He was intensely aware of her nearness. The sheen of her hair, brought out by the hanging lamps over her kitchen bar.

It was happening again. That secret heat, igniting. Her smile faded, replaced by caution. "Marcus," she whispered. It was probably meant to be a warning tone, but it was so soft, it sounded like an invitation.

Back off, Moss. Don't.

He clenched his hands into fists, tearing his gaze from her face.

It landed on her bar, where a tea tray was displayed. It held packs of teas in a mug, a sugar bowl and a crock of pale golden honey. A distraction. He seized on it.

"Is that Corzo honey?" he asked.

Eve glanced around. "Yes, it is. Only kind I use."

"Can I try it?"

"Of course." She opened the pot. The honey shone, limpid and backlit, like a gem. She dipped in a coffee spoon and held it out to him. "Here."

He reached for it. Her hand flashed forward, catching the errant drops that fell from the spoon.

"Oops," she murmured. "It never crystallizes."

Marcus dipped his finger in the spoon and tasted it. Aromatic. Exotic. When he opened his eyes, Eve waited expectantly.

"So?" she prompted. "What do you think?"

"It's complex," he said. "Flowery. Delicate, but strong." *Like you.*

She looked pleased. "I think so, too."

Marcus tried another dab. "I'm tasting the culmination of all your hard work," he said. "Distilled into golden drops of sweet elixir."

She laughed. "I just tweaked some details. The plants, the sun and the bees did the heavy lifting."

"It only exists because of you."

The impulse overcame him. He took her hand, lifted her honey-smeared fingertip and pulled it into his mouth. Images thundered through his mind of licking honey off all of her secret female parts. Leaving no part unlicked, unkissed.

She didn't pull away. She was flushed, eyes dilated, with a dazed glow of arousal. His heart galloped.

"Sorry," he said hoarsely. "The honey. It got to me."

Marcus swirled his fingertip into the sticky spoon and lifted it to her lips. Painting them with honey until they shone, parted, pink. Glossy.

Her breath was ragged as he leaned closer. His lips inches from hers. She could feel his heat. He waited for the sign, alert for any subtle form that it might take. That countermove from her that said *yes, go for it*.

Her hand came up, settling on his chest, fingers digging into the fabric. Pulling him closer. There it was. It unleashed him.

He pulled her close and kissed her.

Eight

The tangy sweetness of Corzo honey on Marcus's mouth melted all her barriers. Her mouth opened as her body leaned into his. Twining, clinging. Arms, legs. Clutching his nape, sliding over his jacket, gripping his shirt. Buttons, scraping against her knuckles.

She wanted to rip them open. Feel hot, bare skin.

Her skirt was stretchy but too snug to wrap her legs around his. That problem was swiftly solved when he shifted her around and moved her toward the couch.

Her legs hit the cushions. She sat, abruptly. He knelt in front of her, still kissing, stroking the sides of her thighs. Every stroke released a torrent of excitement.

She glowed, melted, opened. She didn't remember pushing her skirt up, but up it went.

He shifted her again, and she was on her back. He arched over her, his mouth hot against her throat.

Her legs wrapped around him without hesitation. She arched, pressing her chest against his, wriggling to get him right where she desperately wanted him to be, with the hot bulge in the front of his pants pressing her intimate parts. Caressing and teasing. Promising more.

More. She'd never hungered for it like this. His lips felt so good, every sensual kiss and touch leaving a trail of bright pleasure in its wake. Excitement cascading through her body at every caress, every stroke.

His body covered hers. He ground his weight against her, making her squeeze him closer. She was so enthralled, she forgot everything. He filled her senses.

Marcus pinned her body into the cushions with each sensual pulse of his hips. Pleasure bloomed and surged, more intense every time, until it reached a tipping point and overflowed, flooding her with delight.

Long, wrenching, utterly perfect. It left her speechless. A soft, liquid glow.

Sometime later, she drifted back to conscious awareness. Marcus was poised on top of her, nuzzling her throat. Sara's words echoed in her head. *Will he nail you out of habit?* He could, and she would love it. It would rock her world.

Then he'd get up, straighten his clothes and walk out the door, heading back to his ordinary life and his stable of lovers, which he had every right to enjoy. And she would have officially added her name to that long list. One of the many.

She'd signed a piece of paper the other day, formally stating that she would be fine with him conducting his private life as he pleased.

But if she did this, she would feel bereft and stupid and used. She couldn't do that to herself.

Marcus finally spoke. "Beautiful."

"Marcus," she faltered. "I…that was…my God."

"I know, right?" His hand cupped her bottom, tracing the edge of her lace panties with his fingertip. "You go up like a torch. It's amazing." His slow, dragging kisses made her catch her breath. "Of course it's your choice, but my hottest fantasy right now would be to watch you come, oh, maybe eight or ten times more. Each time wearing fewer and fewer articles of clothing, until I finally get to the hot, sweet, wet, secret parts. When they're completely bare, I'll paint them with Corzo honey and lick them clean. It would take a very long time to get it all off."

The image made her weak with arousal. The man could sweet-talk her into a state of quivering surrender without ever touching her.

"Do you have a playbook you follow for this kind of thing?" she asked.

He lifted his head, a frown in his eyes. "In a general sense, yes. I take care to be sure my partner is satisfied. Why does it sound like you're judging me for it?"

"I'm not. I just… I just can't believe this happened. That it went so far, so fast. My brain can't catch up with my body."

"I followed your cues, Eve." His voice was guarded.

"Of course you did. But I'm having second thoughts. About how smart this is."

He lifted himself off her body. "I'm sorry if this was a disappointment," he said. "It seemed like you were having a good time."

"I was. You didn't misread anything. But I'm not the type who can, ah…do this."

"Type?" He got to his feet, tucking his shirt back in. "What type is that?"

"You know," she faltered. "Someone who can have casual sex for the pure enjoyment of it. There is nothing wrong with that, believe me. I truly wish that I could. I'd have so much more fun. But I'm the kind of person who…" Her voice trailed off.

"Who what?" He had his back to her as he shrugged his jacket back on.

"Who takes it all so damn seriously," she said.

"Whereas I'm the type who takes nothing seriously?"

The controlled anger in his voice chilled her. "You go through women very fast," she pointed out. "My understanding was that you married me so that you could fulfill your grandmother's requirement while still being free to continue that lifestyle. That was the substance of the paper that I signed the other day, anyway, right?"

He made an impatient sound. "We had to cover all contingencies."

"I know that. But we didn't cover the contingency of becoming lovers ourselves."

He shook his head. "It flashed through my mind, but I decided not to say it out loud in front of a bunch of MossTech lawyers. It seemed presumptuous, and potentially embarrassing to you."

"Um, yes, it would have been embarrassing," she admitted. "But whether we stipulated it or not, I'm just not wired that way. I just can't do it."

"Then what happened here?" he asked. "It seemed like you wanted this."

She shook her head. "It's confusing. When you start your sexy hoodoo routine—"

He let out a bark of laughter. "Sexy hoodoo?"

"Sorry, but that's how it feels," she said helplessly. "And I just can't."

"I'm sorry I put you in the position of having to say that," he said.

"It really was a great evening," she said. "I'm sorry if I made you think—"

"Don't apologize," he said. "I stepped over the line. I said it wouldn't happen again, and it did. That's unacceptable. But I've learned my lesson."

Her chin tilted. "Good night, then. Don't keep your driver waiting. Though no doubt he's used to it."

He spun around. "What is that supposed to mean?"

"Don't they drive you to your trysts and wait outside until you're done? And then drive you home? I bet you never stay the whole night."

"I don't see what my past trysts have to do with you," he said.

"They don't." She was ashamed of herself for scolding him. "I'm sorry we hit this wall. But maybe it's better we hit it sooner than later."

"Maybe." He pulled on his long coat. "I'll keep my distance. And my word. Unless you've changed your mind. I hope this doesn't change our agreement."

"No," she said. "I'm still ready to do my part."

"Thank you." His tone was stiff. "You'll have to accompany me to Jack and Maddie's wedding, but I'll stay away from you before that."

"Marcus, I didn't mean to—"

"I'll text you the details. And book you a room at the Lodge. Can I order a car to take you to Triple Falls? It's a two-hour drive in the mountains, so it's probably best."

"I prefer to come in my own car," she said.

"As you like. I'll give you all the space you need."

The front door clicked shut behind him, and Eve sank onto the couch, her knees too weak to hold her up. She could see her reflection in the picture window, over the tufts of Corzo. Her hair all wild and lopsided. A curl stuck to the side of her face. She tried to brush it away and realized that her hot face was sticky with honey.

Salt mixed with the sweet as she melted into startled tears.

Nine

"Here's the key fob for your room door, Mr. Moss." The Triple Falls Lodge concierge passed him the device. "Hold it to the sensor until the light turns green. Have a wonderful stay and congratulations."

"Thank you," Marcus said. "Could you tell me if my wife has checked in?"

The guy blinked, unable to process the question. "Ah…"

"We arrived separately. I booked adjoining rooms. Eve Seaton. Has she arrived?"

"One moment." The man had recovered his professional aplomb. His fingers flew on the keyboard. "Yes, she has. Ms. Seaton checked into the adjoining room two hours ago. Shall I, ah, call her room to tell her that you've arrived?"

The guy still looked puzzled, as well he might. Why

hadn't Marcus texted the woman, like a normal husband would? A simple *Hey, babe, have you checked in yet?*

What was wrong with him? Did he have no phone? No fingers?

Nope, just no nerve. He was afraid to send a text message to his own wife.

He'd tried. He'd composed countless messages. *I'm so sorry about what happened. Could we have a do-over? I hope we can still be friends. I promise it will never happen again.*

Yeah. He'd made that promise before. It scared him that he'd been unable to keep from breaking it.

He stabbed the button on the elevator with a muffled obscenity. He didn't blame her for avoiding an awkward two-hour car trip with him, or for wanting her own car in case she needed to make a quick escape. He had only himself to blame.

It was hard to look forward to celebrating his little sister's wedding under these circumstances, but lucky for him, Maddie and Jack were both too madly in love with each other to notice if her brother was sulking. He unlocked his room door and entered his luxurious hotel room, eying the connecting door as if a tiger lurked behind it.

He hung his coat, and moved toward the bathroom, which shared a wall with the bathroom of the adjoining room, and stood still. Listening. What was that humming sound? The shower? He leaned forward. No, not running water. That was the roar of a blow-dryer.

The images took over his brain. Eve, pink and damp and naked and seductively beautiful, in front of a foggy bathroom mirror, her luxurious dark hair flying around her head like a flag. All her bottles and lotions spread out over the bathroom counter, adding their sweet scents to hers. It aroused him to the point of pain.

A knock on the door startled him, and he jumped back as if he'd been slapped.

"Who is it?"

"Your bags, sir."

His heart was galloping, and his face was as red as if he'd been caught peeping. He strode to the door, jerked it open and dug out a generous tip, shutting the door on the young man's effusive thanks.

He had to coordinate with Eve. To talk to the woman. Or at least text her, since she was probably still naked. And rosy. And wet. God help him.

He sat on the bed and opened her contact.

The wedding starts at six. There's a processional to open the party, then dinner, dancing and then the ceremony at 11:30. Can we go down together?

He sat there, staring at his phone like an idiot, until he saw the dots that indicated that she was typing back.

Of course. Shall we go meet at 5:45? Earlier?

Let's go at 5:35, so I can introduce you to my grandmother, he replied. I'll knock when it's time.

I'll be ready. See you then.

Less than an hour from now. He tried to relax in the shower. Took his time with the shave, aftershave, deodorant.

He examined his tux-clad self in the mirror, hoping

his inner agitation would not show. He looked the same as always, but the constant struggle to control himself had turned his face into a mask.

He looked stiff, humorless, tense. No fun at all.

He glanced at his watch. Four minutes. The seconds crawled by. He pulled the box out that contained the gift he'd bought for Eve. He was nervous about that, too. If she'd think that he was stepping over the line once again by offering it.

Enough waffling. He slid the key fob and phone into his pocket, went into the hall and knocked on her door.

"Marcus? Is that you?"

"Yes, it's me," he replied.

"Be right there. Just a second… This damn thing is driving me wild."

He was jealous of whatever drove her wild. That should be his job. He'd do it so wickedly well. He stomped that thought as best he could.

Then her door opened, and so did his mouth.

Eve looked spectacular in a strapless crimson gown that rustled and gleamed. A tight-boned corset-style top highlighted her perfect breasts, accentuating the luscious valley of cleavage between them, and the dress had a full, poufy skirt. The deep scarlet color made her glow like a pearl. She wasn't wearing glasses, and her big gray eyes seemed even more striking, highlighted with shadow and shimmer and those insanely long, thick lashes. Her lips were a hot red, and her ringlets had been blown out into a glossy, luxurious mane of long, loose curls.

"Marcus?" The way she said his name sounded like it wasn't the first time she'd said it. "Marcus, are you okay? Earth to Marcus?"

"Sorry," he said. "I was just… You look incredible."

She gave him a luminous smile. "Thank you. I decided, no specs tonight, I'm bringing back the contact lenses, but only for special occasions."

"You look great either way," he assured her.

Another gorgeous smile was his reward for that comment. "The dress is a winner," she said. "I absolutely love it. And Federica was wonderful. She wouldn't tell me how much it cost you, but I priced some comparable ones, and oh my God, Marcus."

He tried swallowing, but his throat was dry. "Worth every last penny."

"Insanely extravagant," she said. "On the plus side, I feel like a princess from an old fairy tale on my way to the king's palace."

"That's exactly how you look," he said. "And the hair, whoa. You can make it look like that by yourself?" He almost reached out to touch a gleaming lock. Stopped himself in time. *Boundaries.*

She laughed. "Blowouts are hard to do. I called the hotel last week and tried to schedule a hairdresser before the reception. First, they told me everyone was booked. Then, I pulled the 'I am Mrs. Marcus Moss' card. Everything changed. Hell of a thing."

He reflected that the cat could be out of the bag at this point, regarding his married state, if the concierge or the hairdresser mentioned anything to his family members. But whatever. "Good," he said. "Use that card anytime you can. It's yours for the using."

"Cool. So the woman they recommended did a great job." Eve tossed her hair, which gleamed as it slid over her shoulders, the curls bouncing at the small of her back. "I should have asked her to stay a little longer to help with the dress, which is a pain in the ass to fasten on my own. I got the hooks into the right place, but this dress has thirty silk-covered buttons, and I am not a contortionist. I was wondering if you could, um..." She tilted her head, looking up from under her lashes. "...help a girl out?"

Ha. He'd pay in blood for the privilege. *Play it cool, Moss. Breathe.*

"Happy to," he said, with rigid self-control. "Turn around."

She spun around, shaking her hair forward over her shoulders, presenting him with a new series of sensory dilemmas. He was inches from the glossy, fragrant hair, the smooth expanse of her bare back. Her elegant shoulder blades, her delicate spine, the velvety shadows cast from the overhead lamp, throwing every perfect detail into sharp relief. He could feel her body's warmth with his face. See the down on her nape. The crimson fabric was warm. He got to work, trying to keep his stiff fingers from fumbling. Button after button. Not rushing it. Thirty tight little buttons, thirty tight little toggles.

It took a long time. That magic thing happened to the air. His breath got trapped inside him, the air started vibrating and that intense awareness of her swelled into something unmanageable.

He fought it. His jaw ached. When the buttons were finished, he stepped back.

"Looks perfect," he said.

She turned with a smile, tossing her hair, and took a red taffeta stole, luxuriously lined with black velvet, and draped it around her shoulders. It was trimmed at the ends with a long fringe of black crystal beads. She draped a black evening bag on a beaded strap, also trimmed with fringe, over her wrist, and dropped in her lipstick, room key and phone.

"There," she said. "Shall we go forth and conquer?"

"One last thing," he said. "I double-checked the colors you chose with Federica, so this goes with the dress." He pulled the box out of his pocket and opened it.

Eve gazed down at the square-cut ruby and diamond pendant, shocked. A heart's-blood ruby, set off by the glittering diamonds. "Oh…my God, Marcus. Is that a…"

"A ruby? Yes. I wanted something bold for you. Fiery."

"It's too much," she protested. "I can't accept this."

"Why not?" He held it out. It spun and glittered on the end of the delicate golden box chain. "It's the least I can do. You should have a proper engagement ring."

"Oh, get real," she said, as he moved around behind her. "I'm not really your wife, so this is excessive, as far as theatrical props go. The dress was bad enough."

"The dress is very good, and so is this," he told her patiently. "Go with it, Eve."

"Ha," she murmured. "Famous last words."

He held it in front of her, nestling it in the hollow of her collarbone and fastening the clasp. He lifted her hair free, taking his time. Watching it slide, soft and slippery as silk, over his wrists and forearms. The backs of his hands. So warm.

He resisted the urge to clasp her waist, press her against him. She didn't need to feel that bulge, pressing against her luscious backside. Instead, he slid his palms along the outsides of her arms, which made a jolt of intense energy surge between them.

She met his eyes in the mirror. They looked soft. Dazed.

"Thanks," she whispered. "It's lovely. But you're doing it again. The sexy hoodoo. Please don't."

He lifted his hands away, stepping back. "Sorry. I don't know what it is that I'm doing, but I'll try really hard to stop. Shall we go?"

"Sure," she murmured.

In the corridor, he offered his arm. The swish and rustle of her skirts as she walked was subtly erotic.

Doing it again. Doing what? How was he supposed to stop doing it, when he had no clue what it was? They paced toward the elevator. He tried not to stare at himself or at her in the elevator's mirrored walls. The air felt thick. Hot.

His instructions from Maddie had been to get off at the mezzanine level, and make their first appearance into the great hall down the big central staircase. It was embarrassing, but the bride always got her way.

But considering how great Eve looked, it seemed appropriate that everyone should gawk at her beauty, perfectly framed on the sweeping, late nineteenth-century staircase. He'd wanted to make a splash.

They stood together at the top of the staircase, looking over the crowd that filled the large, lavish art deco–style hall. It had a wall of huge arched windows that showed off the glow of the setting sun over the mountains. There had been over three hundred people invited. It was the wedding of the year, after Maddie finally cleared Jack's name of every last shadow of wrongdoing.

Everyone wanted in on that spectacular and highly publicized happy ending.

But the murmuring roar of the crowd's chatter quieted as people looked up. Everyone stared, and jaws dropped as Marcus and Eve started to descend the steps.

Eve glided down the stairs, head high, as if she were floating. Chin up, back straight, regal as a queen, charismatic as a rock diva. All that was missing was some stage smoke, some mood lighting and a wind machine to lift her hair. And here he was, feeling smug about it, as if he could take any credit for her splendor.

He took in Gran, Caleb and Tilda in a glance, all gaping at Eve. Then Ronnie, giving him a finger-flutter of a wave and a secret smile. Gisela was beaming, arm in arm with her big, stolid husband, Hector. Gisela looked satisfied with herself.

Uncle Jerome scowled with Scrooge-like sourness, on high alert for whatever or whoever was going to try to rip him off. Tonight, Marcus was that lucky guy. His uncle would go to bed disappointed tonight, and that fact made Marcus savagely glad.

He went straight toward Gran, the source of all this drama. "Gran," he said. "Allow me to present my wife, Eve Seaton."

An audible gasp sounded from everyone within earshot, at least forty people. A murmur rose as the information spread via a wave of chattering whispers.

Jerome was close enough to hear it firsthand. He pushed to the fore. "What the hell?" he bellowed.

"Nuptial bliss, Uncle," Marcus said. "Love is in the air."

"From under what rock did you dig up this girl? You think I'll fall for this garbage?"

"Jerome." Gran's voice was sharp. "You are here on

sufferance. This is my grandchild's wedding. Keep your ugliness to yourself, or be escorted out."

Marcus turned away from his sputtering, positioning Eve so her back was to him.

Gran had seized Eve's hands and gazed into her face, her white hair seeming to stick straight up with excitement, though the spikiness was certainly the work of carefully applied styling mousse. "How can this be?" Gran's voice shook. "Why didn't you tell me? Or invite me?"

"It's a very recent thing for us," Eve explained. "Marcus told me it would solve some big logistical problems for him if we anticipated what we both knew was inevitable. So we went for it."

"I wish I could have been there, even for a civil ceremony." She cast Marcus a reproving look. "Heartless boy, cutting me out of that!"

"Sorry, but a guy can't get everything right all the time," Marcus said. "Particularly not when he's being shoved around with legal mandates."

"Oh, pfft. Stop your whining." Gran flicked her fingers at him, and turned to Eve. "Why, look at you! You're perfectly lovely. Where on earth did he find you, my dear?"

"The clean room of the genetics lab," Marcus interjected. "She's a geneticist, working on genome sequencing. A brilliant geneticist. Caleb recruited her."

"So I did." It was Caleb's voice behind them, Tilda at his side. He looked as startled as Gran. Good for Tilda, keeping his secret even from her adoring husband. "I didn't know she knew you."

"We've met, over the years," Eve offered. "Forums, conferences."

"If I'd known you two were close, I'd have leaned on you to help recruit her." Caleb gave Marcus an accusing look. "We could have snagged her for MossTech years ago."

"I was in Sumatra when you hired her," Marcus said. "Plus, don't get your hopes up. She's got entrepreneurial plans of her own."

"Really?" Gran's eyes brightened with curiosity. "What are these plans, pray tell?"

"That's a conversation for another time," Eve said. "But I'll be delighted to tell you all about it when we have a free minute."

Tilda pressed forward, looking as lovely as ever in a dusky rose-tinted gown. She gave Eve a hug. "Welcome," she said. "I'm thrilled beyond measure to meet you."

"Is it true?" Marcus's niece, Annika, Tilda's pretty little nine-year-old daughter, appeared. She folded her arms and frowned at Marcus. Her long dark hair was pulled back with a lace band, and she wore a white, filmy pouf of a dress with a floating tulle skirt, and white-silk ballerina shoes. She held a bouquet of brilliant blue hydrangeas bigger than her head. "You got married without telling us? And didn't ask me to be the flower girl? What's the use of having an uncle if you can't be the flower girl?"

"It was just a meeting at the courthouse with a judge, to sign documents," Eve explained. "No flowers or anything. So sorry about that."

"I'm Annika," the girl said. "So are you my new aunt, then?"

"I suppose I am," she said and laughed in surprise as Annika lunged for her and hugged her around the waist.

"You're pretty," Annika announced. "I like your dress. It's a princess dress."

"Your uncle got it for me," Eve told her. "Yours is also extremely princessy. I'm sorry about the flower girl thing, but we'll try to make it up to you, okay?"

Annika gave Eve a gap-toothed grin. "All right." She slanted an assessing glance at Marcus. "She's okay."

"Glad you approve," he murmured.

At that moment, trumpets blared. A brass quintet started with a loud baroque fanfare.

"Annika, run along with Daddy and Gran!" Tilda said. "They're about to start!"

Annika scampered away, holding Caleb's hand and spilling rose petals right and left from her overfilled basket. Caleb escorted Gran with his other arm, and the crowd was expertly herded by the staff to make way on the red carpet for the entrance.

Marcus tucked Eve's arm into his. He'd been so sick of Maddie's preaching and lecturing, he'd resisted her pleas that he join the wedding party. Now he felt a pang of regret. This was the marriage of his only sister, and he'd batted it away, out of spite.

He needed to be a better man than that.

After a few minutes, Jack Daly, Maddie's bridegroom, emerged at the top of the staircase, his face alight with happiness. The brass quintet blared the processional as he descended the stairs, and then turned around, waiting for his bride.

A beaming Annika appeared at the top of the stairs. She started down the steps, flinging petals with great energy.

Then Maddie appeared at the top of the stairs, swathed in her long, voluminous veil, flanked on one side by Caleb, and the other by Gran, who looked jubilant.

Maddie looked stunning. Her wild halo of black curls was crowned with a flowing wreath of daisies and odd bits of glitter that caught the light, and she wore a slinky dress of creamy ivory silk that set off her golden-brown skin and clung lovingly to her body. When she reached the bottom of the staircase, she kissed her grandmother and Caleb, and then turned to Jack, and took his hand. Her eyes shone with joy, which made Marcus fiercely glad. Maddie was a top-of-the-line human being. She deserved all the happiness in the world.

Jack had better treat her like a goddess.

That dazed-with-happiness look on the bride and grooms' faces did something to him that he didn't expect. A strange, shaky heat, blooming in his chest and his throat. Like something was melting down.

Eve shifted beside him, making a murmur of protest. He realized that he'd been squeezing her hand too hard.

"Sorry," he muttered.

She smiled, eyes sparkling with tears. Which ratcheted his problem up even higher.

Look away. Marcus forced himself to focus on Annika, hurling her rose petals to the left and the right as she followed the red carpet through the crowded room, preceding Maddie and Jack. Gran and Caleb followed them as they made their way toward the ballroom.

Marcus was not the sentimental type. He usually assumed that tears were a manipulative act, because they certainly never came out of him. Now look at him. Fighting tears with all the strength he had. And losing.

When Maddie and Jack reached the ballroom entrance, Maddie turned around, calling and beckoning for everyone to follow her into the enormous ballroom.

The ballroom was amazing. Vaulted ceilings, gilded columns, crystal chandeliers, beaux arts decor, and a band was already set up on the platform at the end of the room. Someone had done a complicated light installation, sending a moving, spinning show of colored lights moving around the walls.

Jack escorted Maddie to the bandstand, and she grabbed the mic. "Good evening, everyone!" she called out. "Thank you for coming to our wedding! As you have no doubt guessed, we are organizing things differently tonight. We open with the processional, then we dance, eat, drink and make merry, and then, almost at the stroke of midnight, when we're all loosened up, we tie the knot for real!"

The room erupted in cheers of raucous approval.

"To that end, let's get dancing!" She put the mic back in the stand.

Jack lifted her from the dais into his arms, and they swept into the middle of the ballroom as a slow, romantic ballad began. The lead singer came forward, a burly bearded guy. He seized the mic with a silver-and-black prosthetic hand. "Congratulations to the lucky newlyweds!" he called out. "Since this is a backward wedding, we thought we'd open the dance with a brand-new original tune, written by yours truly! This is 'My Backward Love,' debuting tonight! Maddie and Jack, this one's for you!"

The instruments swelled, the lights dimmed. The sun had fully set outside, but the sky still glowed a dull pink. A spotlight lit the stage, and a bigger one settled onto Maddie and Jack, swaying together alone in the middle of the room as the one-armed man began to sing in a rich, scratchy bass-baritone croon. The words sliced straight into his mind, somehow.

I loved that girl before I knew her
She spun my foolish head around
Now all my lies have gotten truer
What once was lost is found
I tried to start things at the start
The way the good guys do
But you ran by and stole my heart
Now all I want is you, baby.
Just my one and only backward love.

Marcus looked at Eve. He could see from her eyes that she was following the lyrics. He leaned down to speak into her ear. "They stole our song."

Her lips curved. Other couples were spilling out onto the dance floor, so he took her hand, tugging. "We've been backward from the start," he said. "May I have this dance…wife?"

She laughed. "You may, husband."

Just a dance, he reminded himself, as they came together. Her arms circled his neck and his arm cradled her waist. He held her hand in his as they swayed to the plaintive, compelling voice of the singer. After all, it would be remarked upon if they didn't dance.

And he never wanted the music to stop.

Ten

Just chemistry. Cold, hard chemistry.

Eve repeated that to herself as she swayed in Marcus's arms, thrumming in reaction to his nearness. His body felt so dense and strong. In absolute control.

Every shimmering hot rush of fresh pleasure and sensual awareness could be explained, if one went to the trouble. It was a fizzy cocktail of dopamine, serotonin, adrenaline, pheromones. Her glands were overexcited by the nearness of Marcus Moss.

Cold, hard chemistry. But it didn't feel cold. It felt wildly hot. Her whole body was yammering that she do her part to propagate the human race. That she use the most desirable male specimen she'd ever seen. Biology, dragging her by the hair, insisting that she give her children this man's genes. *Do it, girl. Nail that guy down right now, while you can.*

Never mind that doing so would destroy her emotionally. Hell, it might destroy her professionally, too. Biology didn't care. It wanted what it wanted.

And it wanted Marcus Moss, stark naked, in a locked room, all night long.

It was a constant struggle to keep her mind functioning in the face of his sexy sorcery. It was blasting at her full bore, at point-blank range. His body felt so good. He moved lightly for such a big man. Catlike grace.

After the dance, the band started the opening chords to another song. He looked as dazed as she felt, and she was glad he felt it, too. But that made it even more dangerous.

Biology was dragging him, too. Both of them. Right over a cliff.

After a couple of dances, he got her a glass of champagne, and started introducing her to people. His first stop was a stout, beaming sixty-something lady with jet-black hair and sharp black eyes, magnificently arrayed in a silver sequined gown.

"This is Gisela Velez, office manager and miracle worker," he explained. "And her husband, Hector. Gisela and Hector, this is my bride, Eve Seaton."

Gisela pumped her hand, beaming. "Glad to meet you." She turned to Marcus and patted his cheek. "That wasn't so hard, was it?" she stage-whispered. "You two look good together! She's so pretty!"

"Gisela," he growled. "Have mercy."

She patted his cheek again. "You done good, Marcus," she said indulgently. "Go on, now. Dance with your beautiful bride."

Eve leaned in close when they were out of earshot. "She seems more like an aunt than an employee."

"Yeah, that's because she is," he said. "I've known Gisela since I was a little kid. She was Grandpa Bertram's secretary, back when MossTech was much smaller. She watched us all grow up."

"She loves you like a son," she said.

"Yeah, and I care about her, too. It's a complicated dynamic for a corporate office, but we make it work."

"More human," she said.

"A little too human, sometimes. Come on, there are people you have to meet."

The next few hours were a whirlwind of networking. She met a stunning blonde named Ava Maddox and her husband, Zack. Ava was six months pregnant, barely showing in her empire-waisted bronze dress. Marcus explained that this was the publicist and bosom friend of the Bloom Brothers, so she talked Corzo to Ava. She met Ava's handsome older brother, celebrated architect and CEO of Maddox Hill Architecture. They discussed the sustainable housing projects, his urban greening project, the Mars project and Corzo in the context of all three. She was introduced to executives from biotech companies, to lobbyists, to venture capitalists and journalists.

When she talked to them, it was clear that Marcus had been working on them beforehand, priming them all to be curious and excited about Corzo.

When she met the bride and groom, Maddie gave her a hug. "You're awesome," she said. "You guys look great together. Stick around. You've got my vote."

Eve looked into Maddie's eyes and instantly understood two things. One, that Maddie understood that the marriage was fake—and two, that she was hoping that somehow, it might become real.

That was gratifying, as well as terrifying. It forced her to acknowledge that she hoped that, too. Hoped for it so hard, no matter how she tried not to. Hope made her so vulnerable. This pull she felt toward Marcus couldn't lead anywhere other than heartbreak.

Then again. She would never know unless she risked it.

"Thanks," she whispered. "You're very sweet. You and Jack seem great together."

"I'd say the same about you and Marcus," Maddie said. "Fingers crossed."

Over Maddie's shoulder, Eve saw Uncle Jerome approach. "Trouble on the horizon," she murmured.

Maddie turned. "Ah, yes. Jerome, in attack mode. Don't let him rattle you."

"He won't," Eve assured her.

"Marcus!" Jerome's voice rang out, making all nearby heads turn. "Congratulations. My compliments. She's very shiny and bright. What acting or modeling agency did you rent your pretty dolly from? And how much did she cost?"

"She's not a doll, Uncle. Nor is she an actress or model. Not that I have anything against acting or modeling, but Eve happens to be an accomplished scientist."

"Is she?" Jerome's cold eyes raked Eve. "She can't be that bright, or she'd have researched you more carefully and sent you packing before you even got started. Does she know how short your attention span is?"

"Dad, stop!" Ronnie scolded. "We talked about this!"

Jerome leaned into Eve's face. "Did he even remember your name the morning after your wedding night?" he sneered.

"Give me some space," Eve told him coolly. "You're too close."

"Dad!" Ronnie grabbed his wrist. "Just stop!"

Jerome yanked his arm free. "They are baiting me!" he hissed. "Out of nowhere, he trots out this scarlet tart and passes her off as his wife?"

"The marriage is registered at the municipal courthouse," Marcus said. "We have multiple witnesses."

"Of which I am one," Ronnie said.

Jerome's face went from red to purple. "You're participating in this? To spite me?"

"Dad, please. My cousin was getting married, and he asked me to be his witness. Of course I agreed. You don't have to take everything so damned personally."

Jerome turned on Eve. "Accomplished scientist? More like a high-priced escort, if you ask me."

"Dad!" Ronnie looked horrified. "Stop it!"

"Keep this in mind about your bridegroom, young lady," Jerome snarled into her face. "Whenever you're not looking directly at him, he'll be rolling around in a bed someplace with one of his side girls. Count on it."

"Dad. You're making a scene!"

Jerome turned his glare onto Elaine Moss, making her way toward them. "You and your grandchildren turned this event into a spectacle to humiliate me. And you, Veronica? Playing along with them? I did not expect that of you. Maybe you should spend your energy holding on to the man you have, rather than meddling in your cousins' messes. I don't see him around here, right? Is Jareth slipping through your fingers, girl?"

Ronnie's mouth was tight. "Go to hell, Dad."

"You'll guarantee it." Jerome stomped away, shoving through the gawking crowd.

Eve let out a sigh when the man was at a safe distance. "The dress worked," she said. "All that's missing is a scarlet *A* stitched onto the front."

"Sorry," Marcus said. "He outdid himself."

"It's fine," she assured him. "It's your Moss stuff. It doesn't touch me. Still. Scarlet tart? I kind of love it. I think I'll get it printed on a T-shirt."

But it had bothered Ronnie, whose shoulders hunched as she pressed her face into her hands. "There's nothing I could ever say or do that he would approve of," she said. "Nothing."

Elaine pulled her young niece into her arms. "Sorry," she murmured. "I may have set him off, but I don't understand why he takes it out on you. You don't deserve it. If there's anything I can do—"

"Oh, there is." Ronnie straightened. The smears of mascara made her brilliant eyes look even brighter. "Put me into your marriage mandate. I want to look at his face while I personally slam the door on his fantasies of taking over MossTech. Let me be the one to do that."

Elaine looked startled. Her grandchildren exchanged horrified glances.

"Oh, honey," Elaine said. "I've been walking this tightrope for months. Tonight, by the grace of God, it looks like I can finally step off it, and now you want me to jump back on? I can't handle the stress any longer."

"It's not a tightrope," Ronnie coaxed. "No stress at all. I'm marrying Jareth in a few months. He's asked me three times to go to Vegas and tie the knot early. He'll go whenever I ask him to."

Elaine's eyebrow tilted up. "But he couldn't come to your cousin's wedding with you, though?"

"He couldn't, Aunt. He was in talks for casting a new

film. Please, give me this. I admit, it's vengeful, but Dad deserves it. I intend to cut all ties with him, but he won't give a damn about that. The only thing he cares about is MossTech. Give me the satisfaction of taking that from him, and he can go to hell."

Elaine harrumphed. "I understand your frustration, but tensions are high. Let's let things cool off."

"Please, Aunt Elaine," Ronnie urged.

"Time for the ceremony, or we'll pass the stroke of midnight and make all this a moot point," Tilda said. "Annika, run and get Daddy. He's lost track of the time talking sustainable urban gardens with Drew. Is the brass quintet around? They need to repeat the wedding march. And where did the celebrant go…ah, yes, there he is."

Maddie took the veil she'd removed for dancing off the table and turned to Eve with a smile. "Would you help me drape this again?"

With the help of Eve, Tilda and Marcus's grandmother, Maddie was soon ready, lipstick freshened, veil draped, dress adjusted. She gazed across the room at her bridegroom, who waited at an arbor twined with flowers at the far side of the big ballroom. His answering gaze was worshipful.

It made her chest feel soft and unsteady.

Marcus put his hand on Maddie's shoulder. "Hey," he said tentatively. "I've been dickish lately. I've been stressed about the marriage mandate. But I love you. I'm sorry I said no to walking you down the aisle with Gran and Caleb."

Maddie's amber eyes widened. "Really? You've changed your mind?" She leaped at him, crushing her bouquet in the spontaneous hug. "Let's reorganize it on the spot! Gran will walk with me, then Caleb and Tilda, then you and Eve behind them. Annika goes in front with rose petals. It'll be perfect!"

"Me?" Eve was startled. "But I…but you just met me—"

"You're my new sister! You look like loads of fun. I can't wait to hang out. Plus, Gran is wearing pale pink, and Tilda is in that fabulous deep rose, and you're in that stunning crimson, so together, we're like a garden of roses, fading from white to red. I couldn't have planned it better if I'd worked out all the details myself."

"Are you sure? I mean, won't it be weird, to have a stranger—"

"Not at all. I'm thrilled."

Eve was touched by Maddie's expansive warmth. The Mosses did nothing halfway. For good or for bad, they went the distance.

So a few minutes later, she was part of a wedding procession on Marcus's arm as the brass quintet blasted out the wedding march even more triumphantly than they had the first time. The crowd was primed with food, wine and dancing, and the cheering was raucous. The light designer had put on a spinning kaleidoscope of lacy hearts that circled the walls around them, and a warm gold spotlight illuminated the flowery arbor where Jack waited for them to march up the red carpet toward him.

Everyone was smiling. She spotted Gisela, beaming and clapping. She locked eyes with Ava Maddox, who blew her a kiss. Jerome had shoved his way to the front of the throng. Eve looked away from his icy glare. He was a problem for the Mosses to deal with, not her.

The ceremony passed, lit up like a theatrical production. Heartfelt vows were spoken into the mic, voices trembling with emotion. Her eyes watered, and by the time Jack and Maddie exchanged rings, she had to dig out a tissue to mop the tears. She caught Tilda's eye. They exchanged smiles. Tilda, too, was dabbing her eyes and nose.

When Jack was invited to kiss the bride, the room erupted in cheers. The music swelled, the trumpets blared a Bach fugue. The celebrant beckoned the bride and groom over to the table to sign their documents. A leather-bound folder lay on the flower-decked table, next to a gold pen in a penholder. The celebrant opened it, and his jaw dropped.

"They're gone!" he said.

"What?" Elaine asked sharply. "What's gone?"

"The marriage documents! They're gone!" He held out the folder. "They were in here! They were all ready!"

Everyone looked at Jerome, who shook his head slowly, his lips curled in an amused smile. "It wasn't me," he said. "Incompetence, I expect. Or someone else is tired of your theatrics, besides me." He shook his cuff and looked at his watch. "My, my, look at this. Less than two minutes to midnight. Your stunt has backfired, Elaine. Such a dirty shame."

Elaine Moss stepped forward. "You bastard," she said. "You never were afraid to strike a low blow. You always prided yourself on your lack of scruples."

"You put yourself in this position with your own hands. Ah, look…" He checked his watch. "Ticktock, ticktock…and…voila! My great-niece is thirty years old, and legally unmarried! Happy birthday, my dear. Many happy returns of the day."

"You sonofabitch," Elaine said.

FREE BOOKS GIVEAWAY

**GET UP TO FOUR FREE BOOKS
& TWO FREE GIFTS
WORTH OVER $20!**

it today to receive up to **4 FREE BOOKS**
and **FREE GIFTS** guaranteed!

FREE BOOKS GIVEAWAY
Reader Survey

1	**2**	**3**
Do you prefer stories with happy endings?	Do you share your favorite books with friends?	Do you often choose to read instead of watching TV?
○ YES ○ NO	○ YES ○ NO	○ YES ○ NO

YES! Please send me my Free Rewards, consisting of **2 Free Books from each series I select** and **Free Mystery Gifts**. I understand that I am under no obligation to buy anything, no purchase necessary see terms and conditions for details.

❏ **Harlequin Desire®** (225/326 HDL GRQJ)
❏ **Harlequin Presents® Larger-Print** (176/376 HDL GRQJ)
❏ **Try Both** (225/326 & 176/376 HDL GRQU)

FIRST NAME   LAST NAME

ADDRESS

APT.#   CITY

STATE/PROV.   ZIP/POSTAL CODE

EMAIL ❏ Please check this box if you would like to receive newsletters and promotional emails from Harlequin Enterprises ULC and its affiliates. You can unsubscribe anytime.

▲ If offer card is missing write to: Harlequin Reader Service, P.O. Box 1341, Buffalo, NY 14240-8531 or visit www.ReaderService.com ▲

BUSINESS REPLY MAIL

FIRST-CLASS MAIL   PERMIT NO. 717   BUFFALO, NY

POSTAGE WILL BE PAID BY ADDRESSEE

HARLEQUIN READER SERVICE

PO BOX 1341

BUFFALO NY 14240-8571

NO POSTAGE
NECESSARY
IF MAILED
IN THE
UNITED STATES

Eve glanced at Marcus's face as many thoughts flashed through her mind in quick succession. She was dismayed at such a beautiful, heartfelt wedding being marred. On the other hand, everything might have just completely changed, in a heartbeat. At least for her.

Marcus was off the hook. There was no further need for him to follow the dictates of the marriage mandate. Not if Jerome had already won the game.

This whole thing might already be over. Marcus was free to start divorcing her as soon as his lawyers turned on their cell phones in the morning.

The thought gave her a pang of regret. So she really had been foolish enough to hope that she could be on the cusp of something…well. Real.

"Quiet, everyone!" Maddie took the mic and addressed the room. "I am, as of one minute ago, thirty years old, yes, and you can all wish me a happy birthday later. But Jack and I did not want to leave anything so important to chance, so we were secretly married six weeks ago. The paperwork is registered, and Tilda and Caleb witnessed it. Go ahead and check the validity of our marriage to your heart's content, Uncle Jerome. Tonight's signature was just theater."

Applause started to swell as Maddie stared at her uncle, her smile gone and her golden eyes very hard.

"You lost," she said in a low voice. "Game over."

"Go to hell." Jerome walked out of the ballroom.

Maddie went to her grandmother and hugged her, whispering in her ear. They all gathered around Elaine, who was still visibly trembling.

Ronnie approached. "Put my name on the documents, Aunt Elaine," she said, her voice hard. "Let me hit him where it hurts."

"I'll call my lawyers first thing in the morning," Elaine said.

"For what?" Tilda hissed. "Oh, God. Gran, are you nuts? Tell me you won't."

"Jerome needs to get his knuckles rapped," Gran said. "This is the best way to do it."

"Back onto the funhouse ride again," Caleb said wearily. "God, Gran." He turned to Marcus. "We're safe for now, but I'm guessing that you two will be Jerome's next target," he said. "You're the freshest couple, so he'll see you as the weakest link, and start looking for leverage right away. Watch out for him."

Maddie grabbed the mic. "Crisis averted, people! And now that we've performed our family floor show for you all, it's time to cut the cake and slow-dance! Get in the mood, lovers!"

By the sheer force of her personality, Maddie got the party back on track again. The cake was wheeled out to be admired, and beside it, on a pedestal, a huge square birthday layer cake, blazing with candles.

Maddie blew out her candles. She and Jack took their time with the ritual of cutting the wedding cake, feeding each other bites. The catering staff swept the cake away and emerged shortly afterward, carrying trays of plates loaded with cake.

The band once again began a romantic ballad. Marcus held out his hand. "Dance with me," he said.

She gazed at his outstretched hand…and melted into his arms.

Everything about him felt so right. The way her head fit under his chin. The way he held her. Closely, warmly, but never clutching or pulling her off balance.

This was it. The point of no return. She could not

resist his sensual promise. And what was more—she liked the guy, aside from her gargantuan crush on him. He was smart, fun. He "got" her.

But of course he made her feel that way. He was a born seducer. He was herding her expertly into bed. She knew that, and still, she was going to let him do it. Sweet, sweet relief. She would try not to let this irresponsible choice affect her business partners. She had her team to think of. She would try to hold this thing very lightly, but she was seizing the moment. She would not live her life forever regretting that she'd never let Marcus Moss seduce her. That she'd never flown so crazy high above the clouds, straight up into the glittering stars.

Even if afterward, she was destined to dive-bomb into the unforgiving rocks below.

The energy had changed, after that encounter with Jerome. Marcus couldn't put his finger on what had changed, but Eve melted into his arms as they danced, her tension gone. The band played romantic tunes as the nuptial lace heart shadow-show revolved on the walls of the ballroom.

Maybe it was the magic of the night, maybe the champagne. Lights moved over her face as she flung her head back, smiling. He spun her and gathered her close, and when he dipped her, she relaxed into the move with total boneless trust and abandon before he swept her up again. That unguarded moment turned him on intensely.

If he was even so much as a minute alone with Eve, he'd forget all the reasons why he couldn't do this. He kept on grimly repeating the litany. No vibing at her, no sex hoodoo, no flirting. No charged glances, or tongue-kissing or honey-smearing. No explosive orgasms as she wound her strong thighs around his hips and squeezed herself to sweet completion against him.

The song had drawn to a close. He maneuvered her to the ballroom's exit.

Eve leaned against the wall, flushed from wine and dancing.

"Marcus?" she asked. "Are you okay? You look almost like you have a fever."

Damn right, he did. "I think I should turn in. But you don't have to."

She snorted. "I'm not staying here by myself," she told him. "It's just the hard-core lovebirds out there on the dance floor. I'm ready to head upstairs, too. Shall we say good-night to your grandmother?"

"She went to bed almost an hour ago with Annika. They're sharing a room."

"That's lovely." Eve scanned the room. Tilda and Caleb, and Maddie and Jack, all clinched and swaying to a romantic ballad. "Looks like we aren't going to interrupt them to say good-night," she said with a smile. "Shall we?"

He could do this. Walk to the elevator. Stop at the door to her room. Say good-night. No physical contact, no smile, fleeting if any eye contact.

Shut the door. Then sit on the bed, grit his teeth and breathe.

"Sure," he forced out. His voice felt rough and cold.

Eve almost lost her balance on the stairs, and he seized her arm and kept holding it. "Sorry about that spectacle tonight," he said. "Your introduction to the

Moss family was a true initiation, complete with intrigue and betrayal. We like to keep things exciting."

"Everyone made a good impression," Eve assured him. "Your family is great. What's not to like? They're fun, they're smart, they're interesting. Except for your weirdo uncle, of course. That guy has issues. What on earth is his deal?"

"They say he was romantically disappointed by Ronnie's mother," Marcus said. "She was a lot younger than him. When she was working in Sri Lanka, she had an affair with some guy who was running a MossTech satellite lab."

"Oh. So they got divorced?"

"No," he said. "It was worse. There was a terrorist attack. The lab was bombed. She died in the bombing, and so did her lover."

Eve looked startled. "That's terrible," she said. "How old was Ronnie?"

"Seven, I think. I remember it pretty well. I was about twelve. It was really awful. And Jerome, well. He was no picnic before, but after that, he totally lost it."

"That's terribly sad. You've made me feel sorry for your mean uncle."

"Trust me," he said dryly. "It passes."

They laughed, and Marcus went on. "Gran made it worse by taunting him with this marriage mandate. She's been dangling this prize of finally having the controlling shares, after decades of wanting to take the company in a different direction, and it's driving him out of his mind. It was just nastiness before, but now he goes for the jugular. And Ronnie catches the worst of it."

"She looked pretty wrecked tonight," Eve said.

"She did, yes. But convincing Gran to prolong this

bullshit, just to deliver a moral slap to Jerome? That was insane. On both their parts. We were almost in the clear, and then Gran lost her temper and her self-control. I'm afraid it'll bite her in the ass."

"Ronnie said she was a sure thing," Eve said. "As good as married already."

Marcus grunted. "Yeah, well. Anything can happen."

"I suppose," she said. "I'll keep my fingers crossed for her."

They had reached her hotel room, and their smiles faded.

He couldn't stop staring at her tousled mane of curls. His hands clenched with the need to stroke that hot silkiness.

Eve's eyes were wide, dilated. Her lips were parted, like she was working up to something. Whatever it was, she probably shouldn't say it.

"Good night." He kept his voice clipped, turning toward his own door.

"Wait."

That breathless word made the universe stop spinning. He turned. "What?"

Eve licked her lips, so that they gleamed. "The hotel staff left a bottle of champagne in a bucket of ice in my room," she said. "Did they leave one for you, too?"

"I didn't notice," he said.

"Do you want to come in for a glass?"

He took a moment to reply. "You told me to stop whatever happens when I look at you," he said. "If I go into your hotel room, I'll do it again. You know I will."

"Yes," she whispered. "I do know it."

"We've got something between us, Eve. And drinking wine alone with you in a hotel room late at night? That will not help me control it."

"So don't," she said softly.

He stared for a stunned moment. "Don't what? Don't come in? Don't say it? Don't control it? Orient me, Eve. Help me get this right."

A couple of female guests from the wedding came stumbling by, giggling and casting fascinated glances in their direction, and Eve pulled her key fob from her evening bag. "Come in," she said. "I don't want to discuss this out in the hall."

Fair enough. He followed her into the room.

Eve let her stole slowly drop from her shoulders, like a bud emerging from protective leaves. She kicked off her heels. Crimson nail polish peeked out from the bottom of the gown. Her fingernails were the same shade. He wanted to see her in only nail polish, lipstick and the ruby. That would be a great look for her.

Her eyes slid away from his, her face pink. "So, ah…"

"I know, I know. I'm vibing at you again. I'm not going to apologize this time."

"I didn't ask you to," she said.

"You've changed your mind?"

She tossed her hair back. "I've decided I want to experience…that. With you."

"That," he repeated slowly. "By 'that,' I assume you mean sex. Are you sure?"

"I've been processing since last week. And I think maybe I can pull it off."

"Pull what off?" he said, bewildered. "What is this, a heist? A magic trick?"

She waved her hand impatiently. "The emotional

choreography. I want to enjoy you without getting wound up about you. I need to…to take this lightly."

He realized he wasn't altogether pleased by this development. "Take it lightly," he repeated. "So you don't want to care about it?"

"Well, I suppose," she said, uncertain. "Isn't that how it's done? A lot of my women friends can amuse themselves with men without tying themselves in knots about it. Maybe it's the kind of thing that one gets better at with practice."

"You want to practice casual sex. With me."

A puzzled frown appeared on Eve's face. "Why do you sound so disappointed about that? I thought you were the reigning king of casual sex."

"That's an exaggeration," he growled.

"Then why do you sound so judgy? I'm trying to both indulge myself and protect myself at the same time. To keep emotions out of it."

"No," Marcus blurted out.

She bit her lip. "So… You don't want to do it?"

"I want you," he clarified. "But I want you with all the emotions in. I don't want you to put up walls to keep me out or go to great lengths to not care. That's not what I want."

Eve looked confused. "But how does this even work if I don't protect myself?"

"I don't want a measured slice of you, with all the rest behind a locked door," he said. "That would drive me nuts."

"I thought you didn't want to get involved emotionally," she said.

"I said that before I knew you," he said. "I hadn't talked to you, or kissed you, or made you come. I want to risk us. I want you. I want…more." The words came out roughly. "I want to know you. Really know you."

Her lips twitched. "In the biblical sense?"

"Of course, but not only. I want more from you."

"I want it all, too," she said simply. "But I'm risking more than you are."

"It doesn't feel that way to me." His voice felt raw. "I'm on uncharted ground here, Eve. I have no idea what I'm doing. What might come next."

"One thing," she said. "If you want me to let down my guard, we have to be exclusive. That's a deal breaker for me."

"Is this about what Jerome said about me?"

"Not at all. I spare no thoughts for him. This is a fundamental change in our original understanding. If you want to be with me, you have to commit to being with only me. Are you willing to do that?"

"Yes," he said without hesitation.

She blinked. "Just like that?"

"Just like that. I can't think about anyone but you. I don't want anyone else."

"I hope you're being straight with me, you seductive bastard," she said. "Because if I get this wrong, I'll hate myself for a fool." Her eyes blazed with emotion.

"You won't," he assured her. "I want you. All of you."

She opened her arms, with the sweetest smile he'd ever seen. "Then take me."

Eleven

Eve had half hoped that he'd sweep her off her feet and expertly ravish her on the spot, but he did no such thing. He just stood there, eyes burning with emotion.

"Are you sure?" His voice sounded hoarse.

"Yes," she said. "Life is short, and I'm going for it."

The energy buzzing between them was more exciting than any lover's touch she'd ever felt.

"How do you want this to go?" he asked.

"You are the last person in the world I would ever have expected that question from," she said. "Marcus Moss, famous Don Juan, with all the slick moves?"

"You keep throwing that in my face," he said.

"Sorry," she murmured. "I talk too much when I'm nervous."

"I'm nervous, too," he said. "I don't have any moves. I feel like a clueless teenager with you."

She couldn't help wondering if his intensity, his uncertainty, were acts meant to put her at ease. If so, they worked like a charm. It made her want to soothe and reassure him. Make him feel utterly welcome.

Who knew. Maybe it was a line, maybe it wasn't, but she might as well let his clever magic work on her without fighting it. It was all part of the game.

"One thing you could do would be to unfasten these damn buttons for me," she suggested. "They're as hard to manage now as they were in the beginning."

"I'm on it," he said.

She turned her back to him, and found herself right in front of the mirror, looking into his reflected eyes.

It was a shock to see herself that way. She shone from the inside, her parted lips hot red, her cheeks flushed. The ruby glowed at her throat. The bodice showcased her breasts. That billowing skirt was from a princess in a fairy tale, ready to run away on bare, vulnerable feet. Her naked toes were curled into the carpet fibers, trying to anchor herself so that she didn't waft away like a Chinese lantern.

She shook her hair forward as Marcus started in on the buttons. The corset bodice was closed by hooks and eyes. He tugged at the bodice, just enough so that her nipples poked over the pleated red frill at her décolletage. Her nipples were puckered and tight. Her breath came fast. The effect was intensely erotic, like a painting of a seventeenth-century brothel. The handsome aristocrat, taking his pleasure with his chosen courtesan.

Marcus made a tormented sound in his throat and swept her hair to the side to kiss her neck. Whimpers of pleasure felt wrenched out of her. She pressed against him, eager to feel the hard bulge against her bottom. She shook with excitement.

He scooped up big armfuls of her skirt and stroked his hands along her thighs. He lingered at the bare skin at the top, stroking the thin film of her panties while he nuzzled and kissed her neck. She moved against his hand, squeezing her thighs around it, making those sounds that she could not control. He stroked her breasts with exquisite skill, the other hand busy between her legs, getting every sure, tender touch exactly right, until he slid his fingers beneath her panties and stroked her.

A thundering wave of pleasure rolled through her.

When her eyes opened, her hands were braced against the vanity, her breasts hanging out of her dress, and the ruby pendant dangled, swinging like a glittering pendulum. Her hair hung loose, hiding her face. "My God, Marcus," she whispered.

He met her eyes in the mirror. "So?" There was a note of challenge in his voice. "Are you going to panic, like the last time?"

"No," she said. "I want this."

He let out a sigh. "Thank God. I didn't bring condoms with me, but I'll go find a machine."

"About that. Just so you know. When I found out that Walter was unfaithful, I got myself tested for everything imaginable. And I have no issues."

"Me, too," he said. "I'm always careful to use latex, and I've always tested negative. And I've been tested recently."

"Well," she said. "In that case, I have a contraceptive implant, and it's good for a while yet. So we can just, um. Go for it."

Marcus looked electrified. "Really? You'd be okay with that?"

"I'd love it."

Marcus kissed her throat. "That's the most exciting offer I've ever had."

He pulled the sheet and coverlet off, and started in on his necktie and tux jacket.

Eve reached back, straining for the hooks. "Could you finish opening this dress?"

He unfastened his pants. "No," he said. "The dress makes me rock-hard. It stays."

She stroked the expanse of her crimson skirt with her hands. "This dress cost thousands of dollars, Marcus, even if you refuse to tell me exactly how many," she said sternly. "I intend to use it again the first chance I get. This dress is not a sex toy, you get me?"

He kicked off his shoes. "I won't hurt the dress," he assured her. "At worst, it might get a few creases. We'll get it cleaned, and it'll be ready for use. Pinkie swear. Besides, I'll buy you more dresses. Lots more."

"Don't be silly. I'm not a kept woman."

"No," he said. "You're my wife." He wrenched his tux pants down over his long powerful legs, along with his briefs. Then he shrugged off the shirt, tossed it away and stood there, stark naked.

His naked torso was all lean, powerful muscle. His chest broad. A prodigious erection jutted from a tangle of black hair. Thick and eager-looking.

He waited, letting her look, as if he needed a sign from her to start.

She seized his hand, dragging him closer. She put her hands around his shaft. Hot, hard. She felt the pulse throb against her hand. He made a low, harsh sound deep in his throat.

"Is that okay?" she asked.

"Best thing I ever felt," he said, his voice strangled. "But how about you play with me afterward? I want to make you come again before I lose it completely."

"Okay," she said. "Lay it on me, Marcus. All your mad skills. I'm not afraid."

Marcus pried her fingers loose and sank to his knees, tossing her skirt up. "I've made you come twice by feel. This time, I want to see what I'm doing. And taste it. Can I?"

"I…ah…yes," she faltered, knees weakening, barely able to focus on holding her dress out of his way.

"I love touching you." His voice was a dreamy rasp. "So smooth and silky between your legs. Like the petals of some exotic flower, full of nectar. And inside, oh, God. So hot." He slid a tender finger along the quivering seam of her folds, reaching inside. Wherever he touched, she was glowing with eagerness to be stroked, licked.

He was so good at it. Masterful, gentle, patient. The sensations swelled, endlessly bigger. She would lose herself and never be found, but there was no stopping the wild pleasure that shuddered through her once again.

When she could breathe again, she found Marcus unfastening her dress. "We can lose the dress now," he said. "I want to see you in just the stockings. And the ruby."

She tried to help, but she was boneless, unraveled. Fortunately, Marcus was equal to the task by himself. He tossed the dress away and moved them both so he was on top of her.

"You're sure this is what you want?" he asked.

Eve splayed her hands against his chest, winding her fingers through his silky black chest hair, arching her back. She wound her legs around his hips, giving him a tug.

Now. Her lips formed the word, and he surged forward, filling her.

So sensitized. The slick glide of his body made her shiver and moan.

Eve moved against him as he sought the perfect angle that would hit every spot inside her. They found their rhythm. Just panting breaths, her whimpering gasps. Every stroke was unimaginably good. Every one that followed even better. There was no end to it. Her climax was approaching again; they felt it on the horizon. He waited until she tipped over the edge and let go himself.

Sweet, pulsing obliteration. It swept through them both.

Sometime later, he felt her shiver. "You're cold," he said.

"I'm fine." Her voice was dry from yelling.

Marcus retrieved the sheet and coverlet and fished the forgotten pillows from the floor, slipping one under her head. She lay there, enjoying how his body moved. Bending and stretching and twisting as he tucked her in.

And then, the crowning pleasure, as he slid back between the sheets. He felt so good, so hot and solid and delicious. At close range, his face was even more outrageously beautiful. Every hair, every eyelash, every line. His sensual lips. His erection pressed against her belly. Their foreheads touched as he stroked her face.

"Look at you," she whispered. "I thought you'd be the kind of guy who withdrew emotionally after sex. I was braced for that. But look at you. A cuddler."

"I usually do withdraw," he admitted. "I usually feel awkward and flat, after sex."

"And… How do you feel now?"

"Excited. Happy." He hesitated. "Scared," he added.

"Me, too," she admitted. "All of the above."

She reached out to stroke his erection, squeezing. Sliding her hand along his length. She gripped his shoulders and tugged at him, pulling him on top of herself.

His eyes narrowed. "Aren't you tired?"

"No. You?"

He grinned. "What do you think?"

She shifted beneath him, clasping him with her legs. "I think that you're entirely capable of serving my voracious desires once again," she told him, canting her hips to take him in.

A twisting move and he was lodged deep inside. "So do it," she demanded.

"At your command," he said.

He explored her body, taking his time, using his clever fingers in tandem to bring her to climax again and again as they rocked and surged. After a few rounds of that, she was drenched with sweat. Shivering uncontrollably. Taken apart.

"Are you ready for me to finish?" he asked.

She nodded. Marcus started again, driving her into a perfect storm of chaotic pleasure.

After, she lay there, feeling incredibly soft and relaxed. Clear and bright. Full of light.

They wound around each other, as he kissed her throat, her shoulder.

Damn. So much for keeping it light and keeping her heart barricaded.

She was madly in love with him, and she had been from the start. She was in wildest-dreams, most-extravagant-wishes territory, and she never wanted to leave it.

God help her now.

Twelve

Marcus felt so different when he woke, he barely knew who he was.

He was a bad sleeper, usually. A clenched knot of tension most of the time, and the knot didn't loosen when he woke. The only thing that helped was strenuous exercise, so he ran, or lifted weights, or did kung fu forms every morning, until he'd eased his tension enough to start the day.

This morning there was no tension, just an expansive glow of physical well-being. He felt stupid even formulating the thought, but he felt, well…happy.

Now was not the time to get sappy and vulnerable. But the feeling wouldn't stay down. It kept springing up like a Labrador.

Eve stirred. Her soft, silken heat pressed against his body sparked instant, throbbing arousal. He played it cool, turning to meet her eyes with a smile. "Hey."

She rolled to face him. Her leg was draped over his, and that made his heart and various other connected parts go nuts. He brushed her hair off her face.

"Good morning," she said. "Would you say that this was our wedding night?"

He wasn't sure where she was going with this. "I guess so," he said cautiously. "Why?"

"Then the moment of truth has arrived," she said. "Do you remember my name?"

He laughed out loud at that. "You said you weren't listening to Jerome!"

She giggled. "Just messing with you."

Hey, two could play that game. "Give me a second to dig around in my overloaded database," he mused. "So many women's names. It started with a vowel, right?"

"Oh, shut up." She swatted his chest.

"I'm thinking, an *E*, definitely," he told her. "Edith? Edwina?" He paused, frowning. "Eloise? Ethel? Elspeth? Wait, I'm getting something. Floating up from the depths. It's something biblical, and it has to do with the garden of…is your name Eden?"

"Very funny," she said with a snort.

Marcus stroked her cheek with his fingertip, memorizing the incredible softness. "I remember every last thing you've said to me. Since we first met."

Her eyes widened in alarm. "Gosh. I certainly don't remember everything I said to you. I did a lot of nervous babbling."

"Maybe, but I listened to it," he told her, kissing her throat.

"Um, thank you?" she ventured. "I think?"

"I love your name," he said against her throat. "It suits you on so many levels."

"Yeah? How's that?"

"The original Eve was curious, like you," he said. "She couldn't just accept what she was told. She had to know firsthand. She had to experiment. I'd call her the first scientist. She knew there was a price to pay, but she tasted the apple anyway. It was worth it to her."

Eve laughed. "I never thought about it that way before."

"It's also a story about temptation," he said, rolling her on top of himself, settling her right where she needed to be, her hot, delicious weight against his stiff shaft. "Desire." He kissed her hungrily. "A silver-tongued serpent, leading her astray." He arched his hips, nudging inside. Sliding the tip of his penis up and down…around her clitoris, until she gasped with pleasure, lifting herself.

Slow, hot, exquisite. A heavy, pumping rhythm. Perfection, slick and deep. Eventually, it turned frenzied. Hands clasping, fingers clutching.

They exploded together.

In the giddy high that followed, she snuggled closer. "I tease you about being a heartless seducer, and you respond by seducing me," she observed.

"I'm very suggestible," he told her.

They laughed, with what breath they had left.

"Oh, by the way," Marcus said suddenly. "There's a big post-wedding brunch happening downstairs."

"Oh, God." Eve sat up. "Now you tell me?"

"Sorry, I got distracted. It should be in full swing by now."

"So we should hurry, right?"

"Or we could play hooky," he suggested. "Get breakfast delivered. Paint each other with strawberries and cream, maybe maple syrup. Not as good as Corzo honey, but it'll do."

She laughed at him. "Today is not the day to blow off your family, Marcus. Your grandmother is down there, and everyone you know is watching."

Marcus let out a sigh. "I guess," he said with bad grace.

"I'll shower first." She slid out of his arms and pulled a black velvet scrunchie out of her toiletries bag, twisting her hair into a topknot. "Actually, we have two bathrooms, so you don't even have to wait."

"We could shower together," he suggested.

"We'd never get downstairs, and we'd probably flood the place. Next time."

"I have a hot tub on my rooftop terrace in the city," he told her. "We can go there tonight, take a long soak, look at the city lights as we sip cold champagne."

"That sounds fabulous," she said. "I offered you champagne last night, but we got so distracted, we never got around to opening it."

"Let me distract you again," he coaxed.

"No! Out with you!" She shooed him away, laughing.

Marcus gathered his tux and went to his own room. He hurried through the routine of showering and shaving, eager to see her again. All the time. He'd never felt like this before. He had to be careful not to overdo it and seem needy.

He knocked on her door once he'd dressed.

"Come in," she called. "I'm putting on my boots."

She looked stunning in a clingy knit dress of fading shades of dusty rose, pink, purple. A narrow black belt accentuated her slender waist, and high-heeled black boots jacked up her height, so her eyes were at his chin level. Her hair hung gloriously loose, but her eyes were made up, her lips that hot, sexy red. The ruby pendant looked perfect with this dress, too. It glowed with its own light, nestled at her collarbone.

"You look gorgeous," he said.

"You're looking very smart yourself," she retorted.

Marcus glanced at his dark suit and silver-gray dress shirt. "I have to stay sharp if I'm standing next to you. You were the most beautiful woman in the room last night."

"Oh, please. Nobody outshone the bride. Your sister is a real showstopper."

"True, Maddie's a looker. I know that objectively, but I always see my smart-mouthed, goofy little sister with the braces."

"Lucky you, having her and Caleb," Eve said. "I always thought it would be wonderful to have brothers and sisters."

"I'm glad to have them," he admitted. "And I'm glad that they're happy with their new spouses. It still blows my mind. Out of nowhere, they got lucky and struck gold."

Marcus stopped talking as they got into the elevator. His own words echoed in his head. He may have struck gold, too, but that by no means guaranteed that he could hang on to it.

And whether Eve had struck gold in him still remained to be seen.

Walking into the dining room, he saw Gran held court like a benevolent empress at the head of the largest table. Two places were empty to one side of her. On the other side was little Annika, then Tilda and Caleb. Maddie and Jack were nowhere to be seen. They had done their duty, and they were excused. Free to run away and play.

But instead of resenting them, as he usually would have, it occurred to him that it sounded like a hell of a lot of fun.

He could do that. He and Eve could shift around their work schedules a little, carve out some time and run off together. Somewhere Eve would like. And just play.

People did that, but he never had. It hadn't occurred to him. But being with Eve…well, damn. That changed his point of view completely.

"My dears! At last!" Gran wagged a scolding finger, but her eyes were smiling. "Sit by me, Eve." Gran patted the chair next to her.

Marcus took his seat on the other side of Eve. Marcus met his sister-in-law's eyes, then his brother's, as the server poured out their coffee. Both were smiling in a way that made him feel like he'd walked into the dining room naked. "What?" he demanded. "What's the look?"

"You look so relaxed." Tilda and Caleb smiled at each other like fools.

"I'm half asleep," Marcus said defensively. "Late night."

"I bet it was," Caleb murmured.

"Do not embarrass her," Marcus said in soft, menacing tones.

"We would never," Tilda told him solemnly. "Just let us be pleased for you, okay? Is that so much to ask?"

He checked to see if Eve was following, but she was leaning toward Gran, deep in conversation. "It's not too much to ask, no," he said. "It's just too soon to ask. Don't jinx me."

Caleb nodded. "Gotcha."

Marcus stood. "I need fuel," he said. "Can I get you a plate?"

"Sure, thanks," Eve said. "Anything is fine. It all looks good."

"Yes, run along, Marcus. Eve was telling me all about Corzo," Gran said. "What a marvelous project. Go on, dear. Honeybees, you were saying? Good heavens. That's delightful."

"Yes, that part was a real surprise, at first." Eve turned to his grandmother.

Marcus left them to it, and headed toward the lavish buffet, loading both their plates. Artichoke and egg pastry, buttermilk pancakes, link sausages, bacon and a bowl of fresh raspberries with a dollop of cream. A good beginning.

A server took the plates away as soon as he finished loading them, and accompanied him to the table, but Teresa Haber stepped suddenly into his path.

She smiled brightly, feigning surprise. "Oh, Marcus! It's you!"

"Good morning, Teresa."

Teresa wore a tight leather miniskirt. A low-cut, fluffy white mohair sweater clung to her lush figure and showed a lot of cleavage.

"You look well, Marcus," Teresa said. "Married life suits you. Where on earth did you find that girl?"

"In a lab," he said.

"Oh, I see! So you fell in love with her brain, then? Aw. That's sweet."

Marcus let his polite smile fade to nothing and kept calmly looking at her, long enough to make her uncomfortable. "Enjoy your breakfast, Teresa," he said.

She tossed her hair and flounced away.

Caleb joined him. "She looks pissed," he said. "Drama?"

"Why would there be?" Marcus said. "I never led her on. Who invited her?"

"Beats the hell out of me. She wasn't on Jack's or Maddie's guest list. Maybe she was somebody's plus-one."

Back at the table, Eve looked at her plate, startled. "Wow, yum. Decadent excess!"

"Always," he murmured. "It's just who I am."

She met his eyes, and he gave her a teasing smile. "Okay, fine. You got me," he said. "That's just a mask to hide my tender inner self, but don't tell anyone. Let it be our little secret."

She giggled and took a bite of pancake. "I've never been so hungry in my life."

"Eve's been telling me how she developed Corzo," Gran said.

"Yeah, I was impressed by Corzo, too," he said. "Where are Maddie and Jack?"

"They left early to catch a plane. I think they were heading to Brazil. That enormous waterfall, you know the one?"

"Oh, yes!" Eve's eyes lit. "Iguazu Falls? I would love to see that someday!"

"Let's go," Marcus said on impulse.

She looked startled. "Uh… Are we maybe getting ahead of ourselves?"

"That's our shtick. Backward love, right?" He hummed the refrain to her.

"Marcus," Gran murmured. "Look at you. Giggling. Humming, for goodness' sake. You're positively giddy this morning."

"Gran, please," he said wearily.

"I'm thrilled to see you having a good time. Why don't you two have your own honeymoon? You cheated us all out of a proper wedding, so at the very least, you should take a proper honeymoon. Organize it right away!"

"Well, it's not so simple," Eve said. "I need to work, and so does Marcus, right?"

"I could probably clear my schedule," Marcus said blandly.

"Maybe you could, but I've only been in this job for a couple of months, so it seems a bit presumptuous."

"Eve," Gran said delicately. "I love you to pieces for making me say this. But Caleb and Marcus are your boss's boss's bosses. You can go wherever you like, whenever you like. Discreetly, of course. Without rubbing it in anyone's face."

"Ahhh…" Eve dabbed at her lips with a napkin and shot a panicked look at Marcus. "We'll talk about this later, okay?"

"Sure," he said. "Iceland would be fun. The Galapagos. The Andes. Or Europe."

"Don't leave quite yet," Caleb told them. "I was talking to Galen Landis yesterday, like you asked me to." He looked at Eve. "The Landis Forum. You know it?"

"Oh, yes," Eve said. "We were going to present Corzo there last year, but things went south right about then, so I didn't get the paperwork in. I was hoping for next year."

"Nope," Caleb said, with satisfaction. "You and your team are going. Landis wants you to present Corzo at the forum. Yours is the very first presentation."

Eve's jaw dropped. "But we missed the deadline! We can't possibly…"

"Do you have a presentation prepared?" Caleb asked.

"Of course!"

"So go," he said. "They're waiting for you. It's all set."

"I'm sure you can get your team together in time," Marcus said. "Why not?"

"It's all happening faster than my brain can keep up," Eve said faintly.

Tilda patted her arm. "Welcome to the Moss family," she said. "Like being run over by a train, but in a good way."

"Where is the Landis Forum this year?" Gran asked.

"At the coast," Caleb said. "At Paradise Point."

"Great." Marcus looked over at her. "Paradise Point is a luxury resort on the Washington coast designed by Drew, my architect friend that you met last night," he said. "It's beautiful. It has a Michelin-star restaurant, too."

"And since you'll be going to Paradise Point, there's no reason not to take some time to enjoy your new beach home right near Carruthers Cove, right?" Gran said with satisfaction. "At long last, I can get rid of that last property!"

Eve looked around at them all, bewildered. "What property?"

Marcus rolled his eyes. "Gran bought three houses on the coast, as future wedding presents for the three of us. Up on the bluff. Ocean view. Private beach."

"And that sulky ingrate hasn't even been to see his!" Gran scolded.

"It didn't belong to me, Gran, and I figured it never

would, so why torture myself?" Marcus told her. "At the time, I had no intention of playing along."

"And then you found this treasure." Gran leaned over to kiss Eve's cheek. "You've been saved in the nick of time, in the best possible way."

"We took a look at your house," Tilda told them. "It's really stunning."

"Yeah, we peeked!" Annika said. "It's pretty. Totally different than ours or Aunt Maddie's, but just as nice. Well, almost. Ours is definitely the best."

"Annika," Tilda said sternly. "That's rude."

"Why?" Annika asked, her eyes innocently wide. "They never even saw it yet!"

"Still rude," Tilda insisted.

"Sorry," Annika said cheerfully. "But it really is pretty. It's definitely got the best trees. The trees are, like, huge."

Eve turned to Marcus, startled. "A beachfront house? As a wedding present?"

"Gran's just like that. She shoves her grandkids face-first into matrimony, and showers them with luxuries as a reward. It's very twisted."

"Hush," Gran said crisply. "It's an investment, and part of your inheritance. It's also an investment in your future work-life balance. Caleb and Tilda and Annika go all the time. It's good for them. I'm sure it'll be good for Jack and Maddie, too."

"Convenient that it's ten miles away from the Paradise Point resort," Caleb pointed out. "It'll be the perfect staging area for your team."

Gisela strolled by and patted Marcus on the shoulder. "Good morning," she said. "Great party last night, eh? You danced the night away. Like Cinderella and her prince, except with no pumpkin time!"

"Oh, Gisela," Gran said. "Can the office do without Marcus for a bit? He and Eve need to organize a working honeymoon to present her project to the Landis Forum."

"Gran," Marcus growled. "I'm a chief executive of a multinational corporation. I don't need a permission slip from my grandmother."

"You certainly don't, honey," Gran said indulgently, patting his cheek. "Just look at you, all grown up! A married man, no less! It makes my heart go soft."

"Certainly we can," Gisela assured his grandmother. "It'll be much easier now that the staff isn't always running off for long lunches to do job interviews. Go and have fun!"

"You are a gem, Gisela," Gran told her warmly.

Gisela winked and waved as she rejoined her husband.

Marcus leaned to murmur in her ear. "The ball-busting is more intense than I anticipated. Can we go? I'll take you back to the city, and we'll head to Carruthers Cove tomorrow. Tell your team to come up a few days before the forum to prepare. Gran, how many people can we comfortably host in the house?"

"At least six, besides you two, if people share rooms," Gran told him. "It's four bedrooms and five baths, and if you need more space, I'm sure your brother and sister can help you out with their beach houses, eh? Convenient, isn't it?"

"Spectacular, Gran." Marcus bent to kiss his grandmother. "Couldn't be better."

"No, it really couldn't be." Gran gazed at Eve with

a misty look in her eyes. "Let me give you a hug," she said, holding out her arms. "Welcome to our family."

Eve leaned over and embraced Gran, whose eyes were suspiciously shiny.

Time to sweep Eve out of harm's way before things got weepy. "We're taking off," he announced. "Have a great day, everyone. Let's head home."

"I have my car," she reminded him. "I'll follow you."

Caleb saw his younger brother's alarm and stepped in swiftly.

"I'll drive her car," he offered. "Carlo drove Tilda and Annika here, so he can drive them home, and I'll leave Eve's car in your garage."

"I can drive my own car back, guys," Eve protested.

"That's perfect." Marcus gave his brother a grateful glance. "Thanks."

"But…" Eve looked at Caleb, alarmed. "I don't want to put you to any trouble!"

"No trouble at all," Caleb assured her.

Marcus didn't want to watch Eve in the rearview mirror. Having her right next to him, where he could hold her hand, stroke her leg, smell her perfume…yes.

That was more like it.

Thirteen

Well, look at that. Swept off her feet by a man whom she was officially head over heels in love with, and there was nothing she could do about it except try not to be uptight.

Gisela had said it was like Cinderella and her prince, but with no pumpkin time. Too much to hope. Pumpkin time always rolled around, and the little voice in the back of her head kept on yapping at her to not forget it. The voice had her best interests at heart, of course. It wanted to protect her from disappointment. And make sure that when this bubble popped, she acted with dignity and grace. She would continue to hold up her end of their bargain, as if nothing had happened.

But until that time, she was going to enjoy the hell out of Marcus Moss.

The ride back to the city was fun. There was no lack

of things to talk about, things to laugh about together. The wedding, then last night's erotic bliss, it all felt like a dream. And now a luxury beach house in Carruthers Cove? And the Landis Forum, for her team? And Marcus was so beautiful, it almost hurt to look at him.

She made a call to her boss to arrange the time away. Helen had already been apprised by Gisela, but the woman was reeling to learn that Eve had married MossTech's CTO. She agreed to the time off with no complaint. It would take time to get used to this new reality. Or, well. Maybe she shouldn't get too used to it. Maybe it wasn't reality at all.

But she wasn't going to think about that right now.

When they pulled into the garage in Marcus's apartment building, her car was parked next to his sports car, leaving ample room for the SUV he was driving.

"I'll need to go home and pack for the coast before we leave," she told him.

"Let's get an early start and drop by on our way to the coast," he suggested as he led her to a dedicated elevator. It shot them to the penthouse and opened into his foyer.

Marcus's two-story apartment was huge. It featured a two-story ceiling, with tall French doors and towering solarium windows that opened onto a vast terrace. She gazed at the wood-plank flooring, the curved gray marble accent wall, the big comfortable gas fireplace that Marcus turned on with a tap of his phone. It gave out an instant, cheerful warmth and cast flickering shadows on the walls of the living room.

The furniture was beautiful, in various warm earth tones. An arrangement of comfortable couches were grouped around a low mahogany table.

There was a floating industrial steel staircase with a bronze railing leading to the next floor, where the bedrooms were presumably located. She spotted long hanging bronze lamps, gleaming wooden paneling. And at the far end of the room, she saw a huge kitchen, and a massive dining room table. A breakfast nook with glass on three sides.

"What a gorgeous place," she said.

"Thanks," he said. "Gran and Maddie helped with the interiors while I was working in Asia. But I like how it turned out." He took her suitcase. "I'll run this up to the bedroom and then give you the grand tour."

He returned moments later, phone in hand. "Let me order some groceries for later. How do you feel about a steak for the grill? I don't want to do anything complicated, and steak is easy."

"I'm still full from breakfast," she told him.

He gave her a devilish grin. "We'll burn off all of our breakfast. Count on it."

That promise ignited the air between them. The surface of her skin tingled, as if the wind was rushing over it.

She was flustered, her face hot, and her eyes seized on the first thing she saw on the coffee table. In a simple gray ceramic pot, a fiery, speckled orchid seemed to float, as if it was illuminated from within.

"The orchid is stunning," she said. "Where did you find it? What kind is it?"

Marcus looked pleased. "It's one of mine."

"You bred that yourself?" she asked, impressed.

"Yes, it's a Cattleya crossed with Laelia. It took me forever to get it right, but I love the way it turned out. I call it 'Firedrake.'"

She admired its ethereal beauty. "It's amazing."

"Wait till you see what I've got in my greenhouse." He sounded like an excited boy when he talked about his flowers. "Come on, I'll show you around."

She followed, freshly stunned by an exquisite view of city, mountains, Puget Sound, from every window. She was freshly reminded that this man was wealthy beyond her imagination. Her own mother had come from money, before her father's excesses had reduced it to nothing, but not this kind of money. This was another level entirely.

Finally, Marcus pulled her out onto a terrace. "There's the hot tub I mentioned," he told her, pointing at the wooden platform and deep sunken tub. "I have prosecco chilling in the refrigerator. But I wanted to show you this."

He opened a glassed-in space and pulled her into the fragrant warmth and humidity of a high-tech greenhouse, lit with the glow of artificial grow lamps.

The part she could see was ablaze with orchids of every description. She moved closer, delighted. "Marcus. This is wonderland!"

"I figured a woman who channels nineteenth-century lady botanists would enjoy my hybrids," he told her.

"Show me everything," she said eagerly.

For the next hour, they went from plant to plant, geeking out about nitrogen, microbiomes, water drainage and the challenges of orchid root rot.

"Tilda has trouble with that," he told her. "I have to go regularly to visit the orchid that I gave her to make sure she doesn't accidentally kill it."

"You gave your sister-in-law a bespoke orchid?" She was intensely charmed.

"Yeah, as a late wedding present. I named it 'Love Reborn.' For their story."

"Very romantic," Eve said.

"The one I gave Maddie I called 'Torch of Truth.' The blossom is yellow, fading to white on the top, and it stands up straight, like a candle flame. 'Torch of Truth' is perfect for them."

"Are you going to tell me their stories after all this buildup?" she asked.

"Maybe in the hot tub, after some prosecco has loosened me up. My siblings' love affairs are stories best told half-drunk."

"I'm so intrigued," she told him. "I won't let you forget."

"Great. Come on and see my hibiscus flowers. This is the latest bloomer."

Eve bent to admire the blossoms. They were transparent pink in the center, fading to deeper red, and finally to a frill of burgundy around the border, so deep a red, it looked black.

"I call this one 'Persephone's Secret,'" he said.

"Sexy," she commented. "So did other girlfriends respond to your seduction by flower, or is it just me that's melting down, getting all hot and bothered?"

"I wouldn't know," Marcus said. "Only family comes in here. And my assistants, when I'm traveling. I don't entertain."

"You mean, you never brought your girlfriends to this ultra-mega babe lair?"

"No. This place is my private refuge."

"And yet, here I am," she said.

"Here you are," he agreed. "I wanted you to see my

flowers. It's my private thing, separate from the work hustle, MossTech. They're just for me. No masks."

She smiled, tears prickling her eyes. "I'm honored to witness them. Pure magic." Her eyes fell on a luxurious hibiscus plant, one with no flowers. "What about this one?"

"She won't bloom," he said. "She's holding out on me. Making me wait."

His low voice rumbled tenderly. Then he gently tilted her chin until their eyes met. His warm lips came so close. Still closer.

Closeness turned to touch, and all the sensual promise of voluptuous hothouse flowers exploded between them.

He lifted her onto the table, pushing at her skirt, stroking her thigh. She fell back, propped on her elbows as he slid her panties off, leaving her thigh-high stockings on. She was bare below, naked to his fascinated gaze. He stroked her tender folds, her sensitive, sweet spots, circling, caressing. His touch made her shudder and gasp.

"You're so beautiful," he said. "So hot and wet and sweet. Can I taste you?"

"Yes," she gasped out. "Oh, yes."

He sank to his knees and put his mouth to her with devastating skill. He took his time, flicking and circling with his tongue, swirling and lapping. Driving her relentlessly into a frenzy of helpless delight.

When she focused her eyes, he had unbuckled his belt and was stroking her slick, sensitized folds with the tip of his penis. "Is this what you want?" he asked.

She nodded, and they both groaned as he surged forward, filling her. He leaned over to drag her neckline off her shoulder, kissing the curve of her breast as he pumped in, out. Deep, slow, heavy strokes, expertly petting every glowing hot spot inside her.

So good. So intensely sweet. Every thrust made her wild, rising and straining for the next one. She clutched him, demanding more, breathless. Incoherent.

Marcus resisted for a long time before the pace quickened, but eventually the table was rattling on the tile floor. The hibiscus planters tottered and shook on the tabletop as he pumped himself against her, holding back until she reached the edge.

An exquisite flash of communion fused them. The sweetest sensation.

She could get so hooked on this. Destroyed, when it was finally wrenched away.

Eve pushed the thought away, but Marcus lifted his head, sensing it. "Are you okay?"

"I'm incredible." Her voice was dry, cracked. "I can hardly move."

He pulled her upright. Eve slid off the table, pulling her skirt down. "A quick shower might be in order," she said.

"I have lots of bathrooms, but the one with the huge glass shower cabin and six different jets of water is right off my bedroom."

"Sounds luxurious," she said.

"Yeah, and there's plenty of space for two."

Marcus led her up the staircase and into his room. A king-size bed dominated a vast room with floor-to-ceiling windows on two walls. She admired the red-and-crimson silk Persian rug that adorned the hardwood flooring.

The shower was everything he'd promised. His bathroom was bigger than her living room, holding an antique tub, a vast shower stall faced with shiny black slate.

Being naked under rushing hot water with Marcus Moss ended up as she might have expected. Three explosive orgasms later, she could barely stay on her feet.

He rinsed her, wrapping her in a fluffy silver-gray towel, and rummaged through the bathroom cabinet. "Hang on. I think I have a spare…yes!" He yanked out a white terry cloth shower robe triumphantly, and wrapped her in it. "Hey, I'm hungry. You?"

"I could eat," she admitted.

"We can throw that steak on the grill," he said. "There's fresh bread, salad."

"Sounds great," she said.

Soon they were sipping prosecco while the aroma of sizzling meat rose from the grill. They feasted on fresh, crusty bread, salad and tender Florentine steak. For a final treat, they devoured cinnamon-apple cream tarts as the city lights began to glow. They had whiled away the entire day canoodling.

They weren't finished, either, Eve realized, as he lifted the lid off of the steaming hot tub and topped up her wine. "Shall we soak?"

"Sure, but you promised to tell me about Maddie's and Caleb's adventures."

He tugged her sash loose. "Those are tales best told naked. Hot. Wet."

She set aside her wine, and shrugged the robe off, shivering in the chilly wind. Nipples taut in the cold. "I'm ready," she said softly. Displaying herself to him.

Marcus helped her into the tub, fully erect. Then he sat across from her.

"So far away?" she asked, putting her feet on his lap.

"If I touch you, I'll lose my train of thought. I won't be able to tell the stories."

His brother's and sister's adventures were intensely romantic, even delivered in Marcus's laconic, understated style. Perfect entertainment for a naked girl in a hot tub, overindulging in wine and sex. She listened in fascination all the way to the end.

"Amazing," she said. "So will they really reboot Jack's company, do you think?"

"We'll see. It's still up in the air. Caleb hasn't been sure what was going to happen with MossTech. Too many variables. We're waiting for the dust to settle."

So was she, she reflected. "I love it that everyone got what they were most longing for. Love, trust, friendship. Justice. Redemption. The truth."

Marcus lifted his muscular arm, slicking his hair back with a wet hand and showing her the shape of the silky black armpit hair and the tight muscles of his abs.

"Yeah, they sure did," he said. "I'm glad to see them happy and fulfilled." He hoisted himself onto the side of the hot tub. His thick phallus jutted out. Steam rose from the gleaming planes and angles of his body. "I'm hot," he said.

So was she. Hot and moved by his sensual generosity, his passionate, focused lovemaking. She floated across the big tub, splaying her hand on his belly and trailing it down, grabbing his thick shaft. Squeezing boldly.

It stiffened and lengthened instantly in her hand, flushed and throbbing.

"Eve, you must be tired," he said.

"You provoked me, displaying yourself like that," she

said. "Now deal with the consequences. It's my turn to drive you crazy."

She drew him into her mouth, making him gasp in pleasure, and did exactly that.

Fourteen

"There it is," Eve said. "Number 1204. The directions say, turn into the main driveway, and then make the very first right."

Marcus slowed to turn into the driveway and took the first right. The paved road meandered off through rippling emerald grass and towering rock formations.

The drive to the coast had been as much fun as the drive from Triple Falls Lodge. He'd always avoided getting involved with women he knew through work, so this was the first time he'd been able to talk about his job and be fully understood.

More than understood. Debated, challenged, informed. The woman knew her stuff. It was very stimulating, in every sense of the word. Huge turn-on.

Carruthers Cove left them awestruck. The road curved around outcroppings of granite that protruded from the luminous green turf and then wound up and around into a stand of towering pines and firs. The driveway ended below a ski-chalet-style structure, large and luxurious. Understated, the kind of house you would not see from a distance because it blended discreetly into the trees. A big A-frame window faced the ocean, with decks on the ground and second floor. The first-floor deck had been built around various rocky monoliths that poked through like sculptures, indigenous flowers carefully landscaped around them. They got out, gazing around, and without thinking, their hands clasped. They climbed the steps together.

The place was stunning inside as well. He would expect nothing less from Gran, who had refined tastes and a loathing for compromise. It was paneled with fine, rosy cedarwood, filling the house with its subtle woodsy perfume. The living room had a big stone fireplace, comfortable couches in deep, rich colors, piled with pillows and cashmere throws. Huge windows showcased spectacular views in every direction. In the big kitchen, there was a large white cardboard box on the granite-topped central island.

"What's in the box?" Eve asked.

"Fixings for lunch and dinner," Marcus told her. "I asked the caretaker to deliver some things. The red wines, pasta and bread are in here, and his note says that the white wines, champagne and prosecco are in the fridge, along with the fresh food."

Eve opened the refrigerator door, which revealed heaps of cheeses, fruit, sausages, pastry boxes, takeout containers filled with salads, and packets of white-paper-wrapped fish. "Wow, that looks appetizing," she said. "You certainly don't mess around."

"With food, never. We'll start with cedar-smoked salmon, then fried calamari, fresh clam chowder and pan-fried scallops. There's swordfish steak for the grill tonight."

She looked impressed. "Lots of protein."

"We're going to need it," he said.

"Lay it on me. Shall we look around this place?"

The primary bedroom had an enormous attached bath. Three more magnificent bedrooms also had bathrooms. The wraparound deck seemed to float in a wavering sea of trees. There was a hot tub on a side deck and it released an inviting puff of steam when he lifted the cover. Seagulls and pelicans wheeled overhead.

"I'm afraid to think of how much this place must've cost her," she said. "With private beach access, too. And the landscaping."

"Better not to speculate," Marcus advised. "Gran has decided that being happy and enjoying life's many pleasures is now required."

She laughed at his tone. "Oh, poor, poor you!" she teased. "So put-upon."

"The only reason we're laughing is because I got incredibly lucky," he told her. "It could have gone any way, but I ended up with you."

Her eyes sparkled. "Do you think some things are destiny?"

Marcus shook his head. "I'm an engineer. I rely on what I can measure. Even luck is just a mathematical construct. But I'm glad I had some of it this time around. A lot of it, actually."

That look in her eyes was seductive temptation. "I'm a scientist, too," she said. "And I value logic and reason. But this thing between us…it can't be quantified by any unit of measure I'm familiar with."

He slid his arms around her, nuzzling her hair. "We need to examine the phenomenon more deeply," Marcus said. "Gather more data. Repeat, until our results are statistically significant. You know the drill." His hand slid under her shirt to unhook her bra.

Then both of their stomachs rumbled, and they laughed.

He reluctantly withdrew his hand. "After I feed you, of course."

Eve followed him into the kitchen. "We don't want the fish fry to get soggy," she said. "Shall I put it on a baking sheet and into the oven?"

"Good idea. I'll turn on the stove and open a bottle of white."

They savored smoked salmon on artisanal crackers, bowls of fabulous clam chowder, a platter of tender, crispy fried calamari and four different side salads, and a chilled white wine with a wonderful, flowery depth to it. After their feast, they went out to stroll over to the edge of the bluff, where they could look down at the beach, and glimpse what had to be Maddie's and Caleb's houses.

The dilemma of what to do next was no dilemma at all. They headed upstairs and soon their clothes were scattered over the floor of the bedroom.

Marcus had never had sex like this. He'd had plenty of it since his early teens, but he'd never felt the way he felt with Eve beneath him, on top of him. Her bright gray eyes alight with pure emotion, her beautiful, soft lips flushed red and parted with pleasure. Her slim, luscious body wound around his. Pliant, eager. Exquisitely responsive.

It made his soul shake with something that felt like awe.

The afternoon was waning when they showered and gathered their clothing. Eve shot him a smiling glance as she retrieved her long wool sweater from the newel post at the foot of the stairs. "We've broken the house in, don't you think?"

"Not a chance," he said swiftly. "We have miles to go before we sleep. We have to inaugurate every single room."

Her eyes widened. "Ambitious. This place has a lot of rooms."

He gave her a grin. "So we exert ourselves."

There was enough light left to hike to the pathway that led to the beach. They took the staircase that zigzagged to the beach below, and waded in the frigid surf together, looking into tide pools at the starfish and anemones, their tiny, delicate tentacles waving underwater like petals of green and pink flowers.

When the sun was low and the clouds tinted pink, they made their way up to the house, rinsing their feet with a hose at the base of the deck.

The hot tub was caressingly warm, the tub positioned so that two could sit on the bench under the hot water and admire the spectacular sunset over the ocean.

Floating in the hot water with Eve had a predictable effect upon his body, and soon Eve was straddling his lap, water sloshing heavily around them as her body undulated in his arms and her tight, slick depths caressed his aching length. Paradise.

Afterward, Marcus turned on the gas grill and got to

work on the swordfish. They dined on that, accompanied by the salads and sides the caretaker had left. Then it was time to light a fire and curl together under the fuzzy cashmere blanket with Eve, legs tangled, talking as they watched the flames flicker around the chunks of wood.

The cuddling under the blanket transformed seamlessly into passion. He took his time, making her shivering and wet and yielding before they stumbled up the stairs.

In the darkness, he felt complete, clasped in Eve's arms.

Deep in the night, with Eve asleep, his nose buried in her silky hair, he put a name to the feeling that had been dogging him. He felt stupid, arriving at something so obvious so late. He'd heard the word all his life, from hopeful girlfriends, books, movies, songs.

Love. He'd always flinched away from the word. He wasn't flinching tonight. He was still and calm inside, observing the phenomenon. The way he felt about Eve. The person he was when he was with her.

The feelings opened doors in his brain, and memories flooded out. Other beaches, long ago. Warmer, sunnier ones. Making sandcastles with Mom, when he was three or so. Laughing and giggling and playing with her. Eating noodles and fried shrimp at her favorite restaurant. Swimming in the rippling blue water over the pale sand, his skinny arms wrapped around her neck.

The memory was achingly beautiful, bursting with happiness and love, but it made his heart hurt. For the other memory, brutally superimposed over it.

He's driving me crazy. I have got to get a break. For his own safety, understand?

That had been his first experience of love ending. Like the end of the world, like death. Being unwanted, unwelcome. He hadn't let himself feel it in years.

Which might explain why he so often felt nothing at all. Until now, anyway. He'd been rattled by all those unexpected feelings since the moment he met her. Every interaction felt amplified, significant, poignant. Full of wonder. Charged with meaning, and danger for his heart.

Eve rolled over, murmuring, "What are you thinking about?"

"You," he said.

She waited and finally spoke again. "That's lovely. What else?"

"Why? What do you mean?"

"You were thinking about something that made you sad."

Whoa, that was unnerving. "What?" he said warily. "Are you reading my mind?"

"No, I just recognized the frequency," she said quietly. "What else were you thinking?"

He relaxed his shoulders, slowly. "About my mother."

Eve cuddled closer, her face facing his. She had no trouble waiting for him to articulate the feeling. The silence got bigger, settling into a deep stillness that gave him the time he needed to find the words.

"I had good memories of her," he said, his voice halting. "I blocked them. I was so angry at her sending me away. And then for dying. Being with you brings them back."

"What kind of memories?"

He shrugged. "I adored her. She was wonderful. She was my playmate. She swam with me, built sandcastles with me. She took me out to fancy restaurants. She let me sleep in her bed, when she didn't have a lover in it."

"It sounds wonderful," she said.

"It was," he said. "Until she got sick of me."

Eve shifted in his arms, pulling him into a tight embrace. "I'm so sorry."

"It was over thirty years ago. It's a wonder that I can remember her at all. But tonight, I can hear her voice. I can taste the papaya and the rice noodles."

"Are you okay?" she asked.

"I'm fine," he said. "It made me think about how I've always been with women. Expert at shoving them away. I didn't want to care about anyone that much, ever again. I'd never made that connection before. To my mom. Slow learner, huh?"

"Not at all," she said. "So how do you feel now?"

"All I know is, I don't want to push you away." His voice felt raw.

Eve lifted herself onto her elbow, leaning forward to kiss him. "So don't," she said.

"It's not that simple," he muttered.

"Actually, it is. Simple, but hard. I don't want to be pushed away. I've never felt like this before. I love it. I love…"

You. She had almost said it. But she had stopped herself. Too soon.

"I… I love being with you," she finished, her voice hushed. Uncertain.

Marcus rolled on top of her. "Good. Because I'm not going anywhere."

Fifteen

Eve stared at the ceiling, clasped in Marcus's strong arms. The sky outside the windows was turning the dull gray of dawn.

She'd come so close to letting it slip out last night. Blurting it out would have ruined everything. It was too soon to lay that on him. He would recoil from a strong emotion like that. He was notorious for it.

She'd almost blurted it out, as if the truth had a life of its own. Not that it could be any secret to anyone who saw how she fawned on him, following him around like a puppy, hanging on his every word.

Though, to be fair, he was hanging on her words, too.

Which tempted her to wonder if maybe this affair was different for him. It tempted her to hope for miracles.

She wished she could make herself stop hoping. It would be better if she could just enjoy this for what it was. But emotions wouldn't listen to reason, or consider the consequences. They burned through her, leaving a mess of smoke and ash.

She extricated herself from Marcus's embrace, somehow managing not to wake him. She twisted her hair up, took a quick shower, then dressed and headed downstairs.

The house was brightening with the magical glow of sunrise. So many windows. She made some coffee and slid on her shoes to go outside. She really needed a coat, but she was too intoxicated by the scents to get it. She smelled pine, salt, grass, wind and the sea as she sipped her coffee, watching the surf surge and retreat on the beach below.

Any direction she turned was stunning. To one side of the deck was a gully with a small stream that leaped through mossy rocks as it made its way to the edge of the bluff. The trees and foliage glittered with dewdrops on every surface. The murmur of the sea was mixed with the swish and rustle of the tree boughs.

"There you are." It was Marcus's voice, behind her.

She turned to smile at him as he came out the French doors in loose sweatpants and a waffle weave sweatshirt. He had a steaming cup of coffee in his hand.

"I tried not to wake you," she said.

"You didn't," he said. "I woke and found you gone. I felt bereft, so I went looking for you. I needed to make sure that it was real. Not just a beautiful dream."

"In the morning, I'd never go far without some serious coffee," she told him.

"Why are you awake so early? It's not as if you got much sleep."

"I'm buzzed," she admitted. "Overstimulated by sensual excess. I feel like I've been pounding Red Bull for twenty-four hours."

"I don't see that sensual excess decreasing," he said with a grin. "Unless you tell me it's too much, of course. In which case, I'll back off. In a heartbeat."

"Please don't," she said hastily. "The sensual excess is spectacular. Keep it coming."

"Thank God," he said. "You have no clue what it cost me to say that, but a guy's got to stay classy." He slid his arm around her waist. "Maybe once you get used to the sensual excess, you'll sleep better."

Getting used to it. Wouldn't that be nice, to get used to a thing so delicious. That would require settling into it. Trusting that it was going to be there.

It was too soon for that. It might always be too soon for that. But damn it, she would not wreck this gorgeous interlude in her life by being clingy. Nothing lasted forever. Life itself was temporary, for God's sake. The only real tragedy would be to not live this experience to the fullest. No matter the cost.

At least she didn't have to worry about Marcus being a parasite. He had vast quantities of money. She'd never have to carry him. One anxiety to cross off her list.

But there were plenty of other items on the list to stress about.

"I imagine I will," she said. "I have to relax sometime, right?"

"Is everything okay?"

"Oh, yes," she said swiftly. "It's just, you know. A big deal, for me. All of this."

"But you don't want to dial it down," he said.

She shook her head. "Carpe diem, baby. Seize the day."

"Yeah." Marcus raised his coffee cup. "Carpe diem."

Eve pushed her doubts and fears aside. There was no way to banish them completely, but she still managed to enjoy herself. He cooked a gourmet breakfast for her and then showed her a fabulous game involving raspberries, cream and his clever tongue.

After a long shower, they drove to Carruthers Cove and strolled along the main drag, trying out the fudge and the saltwater taffy, poking around junk shops and trinket shops. Marcus kept urging her to shop for new dresses, one for the final reception at the Landis Forum, another for the gala when they got back to Seattle.

"I brought a dress for the Landis Forum reception," she told him. "I'll model it for you when we get back to the house. It's very pretty. I'm sure you'll like it."

"I'm sure it looks great, but why not let me indulge you?"

"Because it's excessive, and unnecessary," she protested.

"You're very beautiful," he said. "I can afford it. It would be fun to adorn you. I would really get off on it. Indulge me. Please."

She met his eyes, full of patient humor, and wondered why she fought it so hard. As if accepting gifts from him would compromise her, weaken her somehow. God knew, she was already compromised. And she was starting to sound cranky and ungracious.

"Thank you," she said. "I'm...well, thank you. That's all."

"Most women as beautiful as you would invest all of their time and energy cultivating their looks," he commented. "It's a powerful card to play. But you don't seem to care all that much. You're more interested in playing the other amazing cards in your hand."

"Beauty the way the world values it is a huge investment of money and time," she said. "A person only has so much. The day is only twenty-four hours long."

"That's the God's own truth," he agreed swiftly. "So why not outsource some of that money and time and let me drape you in cloths of gold?"

She snorted. "Very slick, Moss."

"Keep in mind, being my wife is very high-profile," he said. "Not to stress you out, but your dresses will be photographed and remarked upon. The designer, the price, where you wore it before. They do it to Maddie, and Tilda now, too."

"Yikes," she murmured. "Is this your way of telling me I need to up my game?"

"No." Marcus rolled his eyes. "This is me pleading for the honor of buying you some hot dresses to showcase your stunning beauty. Tilda told me that the Bon Soir Boutique has good stuff."

"You are a man on a mission!"

"Surrender to my wicked wiles," he coaxed. "Ah! Speak of the devil. We're here."

Eve looked at a painted wooden sign over a walkway that led to a Victorian mansion that housed the Bon Soir Boutique. "We can get ice cream after," he wheedled. "Annika informed me of the best ice cream places and the best flavors. I will share that proprietary information with you, if you give me this one small thing."

She laughed. "You're terrible. Fine, Marcus. Drape me in cloths of gold, then. For the honor of the Moss Dynasty."

Marcus had surprisingly clear ideas and strong opinions for a guy. He also had a keen eye for what would look good on her. Once the shopkeeper realized he'd spend a crapton of money in her shop, she turned the place inside out for them.

In the end, Eve settled on a fitted cobalt blue dress with a tulip skirt that frilled out of the bottom for the Landis Forum reception. Then something caught Marcus's eye.

"Wait," he said, pulling one off the rack. "What about this one?"

He held up a gown of fine, pleated gold chiffon, edged with gold beads. The silk slip beneath was a deep gold, and the décolletage and hem were edged with the same gold-faceted beads. It was gorgeous. "Do you have this in her size?"

The shopkeeper beamed. "It's one of a kind. It might be a bit big in the waist, but I could take it in. Would you like to try it on? I have a matching wrap and evening bag."

"Let's see it."

In the dressing room, the dress slid over her in a sensual caress, dropping perfectly into place around her, and hanging just right. It draped at the bust to showcase her cleavage, skimmed her hips, and the beaded hem had a luscious sway at her ankles.

She stepped out of the fitting room to show Marcus. "Cloths of gold," she said.

"Wow." His eyes glowed. "That one's for the Moss Foundation Gala."

"I love it," she admitted.

"Me, too." He sounded pleased with himself. "All men will envy me."

They made arrangements for the alterations, and Eve walked out feeling pampered.

"Ice cream?" Marcus asked.

"Oh, yeah," she told him. "Shopping works up my appetite."

They took a long barefoot stroll on the beach as they savored their ice cream. She went with the honey vanilla and chocolate madness. He had coffee mocha and pistachio. Icy salt water rushed over their toes and foamed around their ankles. Even his feet were beautiful. Long, brown, strong. Elegantly arched, with long toes. It had never occurred to her to admire a man's feet before. She had it so bad, it was scary.

That perfect day stretched into a perfect evening and then a perfect night. All five of the days they spent alone together melted seamlessly into a blissful dream. Long drives along the coast, leisurely hikes, trips to outdoor spas with steaming-hot mineral baths. Wild kissing on the couch, wild kissing on the beach, wild kissing in front of the fire.

It flew by too fast, and then it was over, and they were planning for the arrival of her team. Sara was the first to show up. Marcus waited on the deck outside the front door to greet her, alongside Eve, who felt intensely self-conscious as her friend ran up the stairs, looking her over suspiciously as if scanning for damage.

She gave Eve a hug. "Honeymooning suits you," she said. "You're so rosy. I like it." She glanced at Marcus. "Is he treating you right?"

"Sara!" Eve hissed. "Don't embarrass me!"

"I do my very best," Marcus assured Sara.

The rest of her team trickled in over the next hour. When all six were there, they sat to a lavish catered seafood dinner. Her colleagues were awkward and shy with Marcus at first, but after prosecco and some bottles of pinot grigio, they loosened up, and soon Marcus fit in with them perfectly. Walter had never been able to follow the conversations when it veered into science, but when Marcus didn't understand something, he asked intelligent questions until he did.

He won them all over, except for perhaps Sara, who still harbored doubts.

The next day, they started in full Corzo-focus mode. Marcus stayed mostly out of the way, keeping the coffee flowing and the plates of goodies filled. He unobtrusively ensured that lunch and dinner happened at the appropriate intervals as they worked.

On the opening day of the forum, they met downstairs early in the morning, and piled into three cars. Eve was so nervous, she practically yelped when Marcus reached to pat her leg. "It's going to go well," he told her. "I can feel it."

She shot him a look. "Thanks, but I'm so rusty. I haven't spoken in public since before the Walter debacle, and it's a perishable skill."

"It's about time you got back into it," he said. "They're going to eat it up."

"Quite literally, if the catering company did the delivery of Corzo goodies to Paradise Point on time, that is. Damn, I forgot to call and check if it arrived!"

"I called," he assured her. "It's all there, and the tables are being arranged as we speak. It'll be smooth as silk. Your research is rock-solid, your team is strong, it's a sexy project. You've got this, Eve."

It was so sweet of him, to bolster her up. But the glow in his dark eyes made her insecurity stab deeper.

Yes, she had this. But what she wanted was him.

Forever and always.

Sixteen

"And so, ladies and gentlemen, that is the promise that Corzo delivers," Eve concluded. "Within a few years, rather than decades, the results can be seen from space." She clicked a slide, showing the satellite pictures, side by side. "These are two pictures of the same tract of eastern California desert," she said, indicating with the laser pointer. "This one is from three years ago. In this picture, you see the same place this year."

The satellite photo from three years ago was barren and pale, while the more recent photo was a luxuriant green. The difference was stark.

"This was after a year of even less rainfall than the three years prior," Eve said. "Add to that the effect on honeybee colonies, the carbon sequestering and the rich soil microbiome that makes the ecosystem resistant to disease and climate stress. I invite you to take a Corzo booklet and consider what place Corzo might have in your own plans to transform our planet's agriculture into something vital and sustainable, offering a future of hope and plenty for all. Thank you."

Thunderous applause. People rose for a standing ovation. The room was electrified.

Marcus could take no credit at all for any of her talent, but he was still fiercely proud. That smart, gorgeous, competent woman was his wife. *Whoa.*

"Oh, and ladies and gentlemen!" Eve called into the mic. "One last thing! I mentioned that Corzo's protein profile was as complete as any animal protein, but I did not tell you how delicious it is. That will be for all of you to decide. My team and I would like to offer you a refreshment of Corzo-based snacks! Try out sandwiches, hamburgers, muffins, cookies, pastries, cappuccino made with foamed Corzo milk, even a delicious Corzo beer! Enjoy!"

Laughter and more applause as the catering team whipped silver covers off the platters of food set up along the entire side of the room.

The crowd surged toward the buffet like a hungry herd to the trough.

Marcus left them to it and started pushing his way through the crowd toward Eve. She was shorter than the seething mass of mostly male venture capitalists who had found Eve herself more appetizing than the buffet, so it took some time to fight his way to her side. He kept at it, a pleasant smile plastered on his face as he pushed through the crowd.

Finally, he was right behind her. He laid his hand on her shoulder.

"Hey," he said. "That was amazing. You blew me away."

Eve gave him a brilliant smile over her shoulder, and opened her mouth to reply, then let out a squeak as he captured her mouth in a brief but possessive kiss. "I practically busted out the buttons in my shirt." He pitched his voice to be heard by at least three layers of the men crowded around her. "I kept thinking, damn. I can hardly believe that stunning woman is my bride."

"You guys are married?" said an aggrieved voice.

A tall, bearded guy whom she'd recognized as the CEO of a med-tech company looked crestfallen. "Congrats," he said to Marcus. "I didn't know you were married, Moss. I heard about your brother and your sister, but not about you."

"It happened really fast," Marcus said. "Once I spotted her, I had to snap her up fast. You know how it is. Carpe diem, right?"

"Lucky guy," someone from behind him said.

Marcus gave them all a hard, glittering smile. "Don't I know it." Subtext: *Don't even think about it, dudes. Let it go. For all time.*

His ruthless alpha-dog strategy loosened the crush, but he still ended up lingering like a smiling sentinel for twenty minutes while Eve chatted and networked.

When the tight crowd eased, he escorted her and her team around, making introductions to executives, investors, philanthropists and venture capitalists. They were stuffing their faces with the catered Corzo bounty, which looked very appetizing, especially with lunch still a couple of hours on the horizon.

Trevor Wexford, a venture capitalist whom Marcus knew and cordially disliked, swaggered by, his napkin loaded with Corzo mini-burgers, a cup of beer in his other hand. Trevor was a short, balding guy with a goatee and sharp, close-set dark eyes.

"My compliments for your presentation," Trevor said, his gaze raking Eve lasciviously. "I'd love to get together and talk."

"There's a sign-up sheet," Marcus reminded him. "You can reserve a half-hour slot to discuss partnership opportunities with her team in the afternoon time slots. There are only three slots left, so I'd move fast."

"Actually, I hoped to get you for a meal," Wexford said to Eve, waggling his eyebrows. "Maybe away from here, so we won't be constantly interrupted by all the people who constantly want your attention. Dinner tonight?"

"We're on our honeymoon, Trevor," Marcus said. "It's a working honeymoon, but meals are mine. Download the Landis Forum scheduling app on your phone, and book a slot like the rest of the teeming masses."

"Marcus!" Eve gave him a startled glance.

Whoops. He was overdoing it. He gave Eve an innocent smile. "Are you hungry?" he asked. "I can get you a plate. What's your pleasure? Sweet or savory?"

"I'll handle that myself," she said in a sharp, hushed voice. "I can handle a lot of things myself. From getting my own snacks to organizing my own appointments. I appreciate your zeal, but you're hovering."

"Yeah, don't hover," Trevor said, sneering. "Callista hates when I do that."

Yeah, in fact, Callista did hate that. She'd complained about it in their last encounter. Marcus knew Trevor's beautiful and sexually adventurous wife very well, since they had used each other for hot, no-strings sex on more than one occasion. But that was in the past, and he never kissed and told.

"Sorry," Marcus murmured. "The temptation is strong. But I'll fight it."

"You do that," Trevor said. He turned to Eve. "So? Dinner?"

"Let's start with the appointment schedule, so you can meet my team," Eve said.

Marcus rejoiced inwardly as Trevor shrugged. "If you insist," he said, stuffing another burger into his face and washing it down with beer. "The beer is like a good German weiss. When you went on about the protein profile, I thought the food would be birdfeed, but these juicy little beef burgers are tasty as hell."

"Actually, it's not beef," Eve told him. "That's Corzo. Not just the bread. The burger, too."

Trevor stopped chewing and stared. "Huh?"

"Mixed in with some other plant proteins, but yes."

Trevor stared at the burger in his hand, blinking. "Well, I'll be damned."

"We get that a lot," she said. "Enjoy!"

Marcus swept her off toward the next introduction, before she had a chance to scold him again, and she was quickly distracted by the task of charming another venture capitalist. The guy was camped out next to the beer table, already red-faced on his third glass. While Eve was charming him, Marcus noticed mini-jars of Corzo honey in a basket next to the coffee, tea and cappuccino station. He pocketed a few of them, and then spotted Annabelle Harlow, a middle-aged lady built like a brick wall, with a poufy mane of bright red hair and a Texas twang. She was an heiress to a massive Texas oil and gas fortune. He brought her over to meet Eve, and predictably, Eve charmed her. Annabelle then took Eve under her wing and introduced her to her own contacts.

And on it went. The day was long, intense. Caleb had strong-armed Landis into shifting Eve's Corzo presentation onto the very first day, so she could impress all the participants before any exhaustion, burnout or cynicism set in. Still, Corzo would've impressed them on any day and at any hour. Eve was tirelessly gorgeous and vibrant. Smart, charming, funny. He could watch her forever.

So could a lot of other guys. He couldn't help but notice. In fact, his biggest challenge was in controlling his impulses to be possessive of her time and attention. That would be childish and stupid. This was her moment to shine. It was her job to charm and impress these people, and it was his job to help her do it.

The whole week passed like that. A blur of constant networking and extroversion. Every afternoon session with the Corzo team was booked. By the time they got back to their house every night, it was long after dark, and the team dropped directly into bed.

Eve herself slept little. She was up late every night, tapping away at her laptop until long after midnight. If he were a dickhead, he'd be jealous. As it was, he dealt with it. He was the rainmaker. The magic man who made it all happen for her.

And it happened. By the final day, Corzo's future had been secured. They had more than enough investors to proceed. Eve's team was very friendly with him now, and he got several big hugs that last day before they headed back to the city.

Before Sara climbed into the driver's seat, she gave

him a fierce hug and a narrow stare, focusing into his eyes. "Keep it up," she muttered.

Keep up what? Following Eve around, trying to keep her attention? Like he had any choice. He hugged Sara back. "I'll try," he promised.

Once Sara's taillights disappeared into the thick trees, Marcus let out a long sigh.

"Wow," he said. "That was intense."

"It sure was." Eve's hand found his, her fingers twining with his. "Thanks for making it all happen for me. You really delivered on your promise."

"I just facilitated. You're the one with the goods."

"You know damn well it wouldn't have gone that way without you. So thanks."

He squeezed her hand. "It was an honor."

They gazed out at the moon rising. "I'm glad it's just us again," Eve said.

"Me, too," Marcus said. "Even though I love your team. We have a few days before we have to be back for the gala. Shall we stay here until then?"

"That sounds great." Eve headed inside, tugging him after herself.

He followed her through the house, still cluttered from Corzo meetings. Up the stairs into the bedroom. Eve kicked off her shoes. "I'm grabbing a quick shower."

Marcus threw off his coat and shirt, and kicked off his shoes. He was reminded of that moment during their wedding ceremony. The panic attack, or whatever it was. Like pressure was building inside him, energy about to burst out, but he had no idea what it would look like when it did.

The bathroom door opened, and Eve came out in a cloud of steam, wrapped in a towel, her mass of curly dark hair damp and fuzzed with misty droplets. So sweet and fragrant. Her eyes were so bright and deep. Her lips so red.

The words fell out of his mouth. "I love you," he said.

Eve's mouth fell open. Her eyes went huge.

"You don't have to say anything," he added. "I never said that before to anyone. It just…did a jailbreak. I know it's too soon. Sorry."

"Marcus, I—"

"You don't have to respond. I know it's not—"

"Marcus, stop." Her voice was crisp. "Let me respond how I want to. Don't try to control my reaction."

"Okay," he said swiftly. "Respond, then."

"I love you, too," she said.

He stared at her until he could speak again. "You… you do?"

"Ass over teakettle," she said. "Ever since that first dinner with you, when you found me at the lab and proposed to me. I've been fighting this feeling so hard. But you make it impossible. You're so sweet and sexy. Fun to be with. I can't resist."

"That first night here, you, are…" His voice trailed off. "You started to say…"

"I almost blurted it out," she admitted. "But I stopped myself. I didn't want to scare you, or be too clingy. I was trying to play it cool."

"No," he said. "I don't want you to play it cool. I want all the heat. Cling all you want. It'll never be enough for me. I want all of you."

She let the towel drop. "You can have all of me," she said.

Just a split second of unbelieving joy, and she was in his arms. Then she was beneath him on the bed, arms and legs clasping him. Holding him. So sweet. Her skin was flower-petal soft, her scent made him dizzy. He gulped it in.

He got his pants off somehow, kicking and struggling. It was her flowerlike scent that reminded him, and he reached into the bedside drawer until he found his prize. The little jars of Corzo honey that he'd stowed in there, for occasions such as this.

She laughed when she saw them. "What's this? Have you been purloining the swag, Moss?"

"I earned this honey," he told her, as he opened one. "I've been thinking about it ever since that night when I kissed it off your lips. I love the taste of it, mixed with the taste of you."

Her laughter cut off into a moan of startled pleasure as he painted her taut, perfect, deep-pink nipple with honey, smearing it until it gleamed in the dim light. "I love you," he said again, loving the way the words made him feel. "I love you."

He bent to suck the honey off her nipple, and she arched beneath him, gasping. He just kept on saying it, even though the words were muffled by having his mouth full and his tongue busy.

But he didn't stop. He would never get tired of saying it.

Seventeen

"Gran's texting me to rescue her from Joanna Hollis," Marcus murmured into her ear. "Excuse me. I'll be back as soon as I can. That Hollis woman will talk our ears off."

Eve smiled at him. "Okay, good luck with it. Later."

Marcus kissed her, as he did every time he walked away, even just to the next room. She followed his progress helplessly with her eyes as he strode away. So gorgeous.

The world glowed with promise. She was decked out in the gorgeous golden gown he'd bought for her at the coast, and it made her feel so beautiful. She'd given in to her feelings for him completely. She couldn't help it. She was entertaining hopes and dreams and longings she'd never dared to voice before. Like children, for instance. When to have them. How many, what to name them. They were leaving for a two-week honeymoon that weekend, some stunning South Sea island that Marcus wanted to show her. Sugar sand, palm trees, pale blue water.

She was practically living with him, going home only to water the plants and get fresh clothes, but she still hadn't had time to officially move in, not with Corzo taking off, plus the time that a red-hot love affair took out of her schedule. The genome project was missing her, too. There just weren't enough hours in the day. Busy, busy.

She intercepted a seething glance from the next table out of the corner of her eye. It was Teresa Haber, whom she'd seen at Maddie and Jack's wedding. The woman's eyes slid away quickly. She was probably still pining for Marcus.

Sara sat next to Eve, stunning in a tight red silk sheath. "Just look at that," Sara murmured as she followed Marcus's progress across the room. "He ticks all the boxes. Smart, rich, handsome, affectionate, a kick-ass engineer, he adores you and he's wicked good in bed, right? Tell me the truth, now."

"Sara! People will hear you!"

"It'll be nothing they haven't heard before," Sara teased. "But as long as all of that famous skill is totally at your service, I guess it's okay."

"He assures me it is," Eve said. "And I believe him."

"Well, then," Sara said with satisfaction. "Great. Couldn't happen to a nicer person. All your wildest dreams. You have some big magic, Eve."

"Thanks. I try."

The room fell silent as the emcee quieted everyone before calling on Tilda Moss, Marcus's gorgeous sister-in-law. Tilda came to the podium and started her speech.

She talked about the many applications of the FarEye project, and how it could figure into the Moss Foundation's philanthropic projects in the developing world.

Tilda was an excellent speaker, and Eve and Sara were listening with interest, when a man walking past stumbled against their table. It rattled and swayed, and dumped a glass of red wine right onto the front of Sara's dress.

Sara jerked back with a gasp of dismay, grabbing a napkin and dabbing frantically. "Excuse me. I'm running off to the ladies' to fix this."

"Gotcha. Good luck."

The man who had stumbled into the table used it to shove himself upright, making the plates and glasses rattle and shake again, and Eve recognized Trevor Wexford. The guy had pledged to invest a hefty sum in Corzo, which meant she had to be polite to him, even if he was obnoxious, and somewhat handsy. And on this occasion, extremely drunk.

"Good evening, Mr. Wexford," she said, hoping his wife wasn't nearby. The beautiful Callista was always full of snark.

Trevor swung his head around. His dark, close-set button eyes fastened onto her face. "Oh," he said loudly. "So it's you!"

"Yes, it is," she said. "Please, keep quiet. I'm listening to the speech."

"You're telling me to shut up? Hell of a thing, coming from you."

Eve gave him a blank look. "Huh? What are you talking about?"

"I'll tell you what." Wexford lurched forward, catching himself on the table once again. "You're a fraud. Your whole project is a freaking…goddamn…*fake*!"

Trevor was so loud, Tilda paused in her speech, casting a puzzled glance in their direction. When she spoke again, Eve exhaled and turned back to Wexford, wondering how best to manage him. The guy was clearly hallucinating.

She should get this drunken idiot out of people's way before he disrupted the presentation. She'd spent enough time with her father while he was drunk to know that a man in a contentious mood would always follow an argument, wherever it might lead. He'd never just let it walk out of the room unchallenged.

She rose and headed for the exit. Sure enough, Trevor followed right after, spoiling for a fight.

When she was right outside the ballroom door, in the large lobby area, she turned around, crossing her arms over her chest, waiting until he followed her out.

"Okay, Trevor," she said, when the door had fallen shut. "What the hell are you talking about?"

"I know, Eve." He got in her face, forcing her to avoid the blast of his hot breath. "I know all of it. Everyone knows."

She shook her head. "Everyone knows what?"

"That you falsified your research! You were going to take the money and run, but we're onto you now. You're a fraud, and a thief!"

"But I never—"

"Ah, there you are, sweetheart." Callista, Trevor's wife, resplendent in a black, low-cut sequined gown, slunk sinuously out the ballroom door.

"Do you know what he's going on about?" Eve asked her.

"Certainly," Callista said. "We heard that your original research data has been altered to look more favorable than it really is. We've seen the originals, along with the doctored versions, side by side. We can't be fooled any longer."

"I never doctored anything!" Eve was outraged. "Never in my life!"

"In the face of all this evidence, how can we possibly believe you now?" Callista asked sweetly. "You got farther than most would, I'll give you that, but you can't fool us."

"I have never tried to fool anyone! My research is absolutely sound!"

"Well, be that as it may, I'll take Trevor and get back to the gala," Callista said. "Enjoy it while you can, because I have a feeling you'll soon be persona non grata. Have a nice evening!"

Eve watched, aghast, as Callista dragged her husband by the arm, scolding him as he tottered alongside her.

Doctored evidence? Fraud? What the hell?

Eve ran as fast as her heels would allow to the nearest women's restroom, hoping she'd happen on the one that Sara had chosen. The room with the rows of sinks was deserted, so she turned the corner toward the bathroom stalls, calling out. "Sara! Sara? Are you still in here?"

Nothing. She turned the corner toward the sinks again and stopped.

Teresa Haber stood there, hyperextending her impressive backside as she bent to apply fresh red lipstick to her puckered mouth.

Teresa turned. "Ah, there you are."

"Why?" Eve asked, in trepidation. "Were you looking for me?"

"I noticed you tangling with Trevor," Teresa said.

"What a slob, right? Getting blind drunk here, of all places. Such a bozo. What did he want?"

"That's no one's business but mine," Eve told her.

"Oh, don't get snippy. I'm trying to help. He was freaking out about the rumor about the Corzo project, right? He hates being fooled."

Eve's blood pounded in her ears. "What have you heard about that?" Her voice sounded far away.

"It's not like I'm surprised." Teresa rolled her eyes. "Corzo was too good to be true, right? I mean, please. It feeds the planet, it saves the bees, and it cures cancer in its free time. Give me a freaking break. You should've eased down a little on the save-the-planet eco-hype. It was way over-the-top."

"I have never misrepresented my research! Whoever is slandering my work is a goddamn liar!"

"Honey. Please." Teresa's voice was condescending. "Ethics are all very well and good, but we all know that the rules change when billions of dollars are at stake."

"No, actually." Her voice rang in the echoing marble room. "They don't change for me. I don't give a shit about the money. My research is rock-solid. Someone's out to get me, and I have to find out who."

Teresa dropped her lipstick back into her evening bag and studied Eve as she smeared her lips together. "You know what?" she asked, in a wondering tone. "I believe you. Which is miraculous, considering the cynical bitch that I am. You're very convincing. That wild-eyed crusader look in your eyes can't be faked."

Eve studied her, wary. "I'm not sure how to respond to that."

Teresa shrugged. "My point is, I think that the buzz about Corzo is deserved."

"Okay," Eve said. "So what's your point?"

"Ask yourself, Eve," Teresa said. "Who benefits from this?"

"No one!" she said.

Teresa snorted. "You're so naive. If all of your investors bail, who's the knight in shining armor who will pick up the pieces, and fund your amazing, game-changing big idea? You don't think people have been scheming and plotting to get a piece of you ever since the news about Corzo hit? Even if they have to tear you into bloody pieces to get it?"

Eve was still bewildered. "What are you saying?"

"I'm talking about MossTech. Your adoring husband. I've seen this before, Eve. First, he drapes you with gold and gems, kisses your hand and tells you that you're his precious little princess. He always does that when he wants something. In this case, Corzo. I mean, yeah, Corzo is a game-changer, and I'd scheme for a piece of it, too. But he's an ice-cold whoring bastard to use you like that."

In the mirror behind Teresa, Eve glimpsed her own face. It was chalky white, her eyes horrified, her lipstick bright against her pallor.

"No," she forced out. "That can't be true."

"Face it, Eve," Teresa said. "When everything falls to shit, MossTech will be there, ready to save you. They want your billion-dollar idea for themselves. Marcus is a diabolical manipulator. I can bear witness. He takes what he wants from a woman, and when he's done, he tosses her. He did it to me. He'll do it to you."

"No," she repeated. "No way."

"I didn't want to believe it, either," Teresa said. "Of course, my time with Marcus was brief. I didn't have any amazing intellectual property that he wanted. But it's the same pattern. He courts you, he squeezes you, he dumps you. I could find dozens of women who could tell you the exact same story."

"No." Eve kept repeating it, as if she could ward Teresa's words away.

Teresa's eyes widened as a new thought came to her. "Oh! Do you know how he found you? Funny story. It's been making the rounds. The administrative staff in his office like to gossip, you see."

Eve braced herself for a fresh blow. "He said he'd heard about Corzo, and he thought he could do something to help the project," she said. "That's all."

"Nope." Teresa's tone was triumphant. "He drew your name out of a bag, like a party game. It was random, Eve. That's how much he cares. And because he's a lucky bastard, he drew the name of the girl with the billion-dollar idea. You were a lottery number. No more, no less. He picked you, and he played you."

Eve backed away. "Get away from me."

"I've said my piece. I thought you should know. Truth is better, even when it hurts."

"I don't trust you," Eve said.

"Good luck, Eve. I mean that sincerely, from one Marcus Moss ex to a future one." She walked out, hips swaying.

Eve bent over for a couple of minutes to get the blood into her head, or she would have ended up on the floor. Her insides churned. Her hands were ice-cold.

Come on, Seaton. No smelling salts for you.

She splashed her face with cold water and checked to make sure her makeup was presentable. Eve stumbled out of the restroom, trying to remember which ballroom entrance was nearest her table, but everything in her head had been displaced by this huge, indigestible fact.

Marcus? Playing her...for Corzo?

Impossible. She couldn't have gotten him this wrong.

She saw a red flash out of the corner of her eye. Sara was hurrying toward her.

Her friend grabbed her arms. "Eve, are you okay? Your face is bone white. Are you sick?"

"Sara," she said "We have a problem."

"Damn right we do," Sara said, stealing her over to one of the ornate antique-style love seat benches that lined the walls of the lobby. "I just talked to Richard Martelle."

"Did he say he's gotten a tip about Corzo?" she asked. "Did he say he'd heard that our research is bogus?"

"You too, huh? Yes."

"I got it from Trevor Wexford," Eve said. "And Teresa Haber."

Sara's mouth tightened. "Somebody's lying ass needs a whooping," she said. "And I'm the one to deliver it. As soon as we pin the rat bastard down."

Eve shook her head. "But how...who would do something like this?" she whispered. "Why?"

Sara's fingers tightened, and she pulled Eve toward her, giving her a tiny shake. "Don't look like that, Eve. It's going to be okay. We'll get through this, just like all the other crap we've gotten through."

Someone emerged from the ballroom. It was Henry O'Calloran, another one of Corzo's investors. She leaped up and hurried toward him. "Henry! Stop!"

Henry, a balding guy with rimless round glasses, turned around, a nervous look in his pale-lashed eyes. "Oh. Eve. I'm in a rush, so—"

"You heard that malicious rumor, right? You got the tip?"

"Ah, yes," Henry admitted. "I did."

"Who was it from?" she demanded.

"Eve." Henry backed away nervously. "I don't want to get involved, okay?"

"I'm not asking you to get involved. I deserve to know who is slandering my work. It costs you nothing, Henry. Just tell us who."

Henry huffed. "It was an anonymous text. Whoever did it sent a package to all the investors with hundreds of pages of attached documents. The originals, and alongside, the altered versions that you shared with us."

"That's a lie," she said. "The research results I showed you were genuine. You're being played by someone, but not by me."

Henry looked from her to Sara and back again. "That might be so, but at the moment, I am not in any position to make the financial commitment we discussed before," he said. "Not until I know more."

"Forward me that text message," Eve said.

Henry harrumphed. "It's inappropriate of you to make demands, under the circumstances—"

"Forward me the goddamn message, Henry. I'm not asking that much."

"Fine." Henry pulled out his phone, scowling, and poked at it. "There. I forwarded it to you and Sara. And if you'll excuse me, I need to get back to my wife."

Eve and Sara both pulled their phones out of their evening bags and hunched over them, heads together, clicking open the attachment.

It was just as Henry had said. Page after page of the research they'd made available to all the potential investors. Each page was placed alongside another slightly altered version of the same document, making it seem as if their originals had been doctored to make the results look more favorable. The way it was presented, it looked very bad for Corzo.

"Even if we go around to the investors one by one to prove them wrong, this hurts us," Sara said. "The project will be tainted by doubt."

Eve swallowed hard as she thought about Teresa's accusation. "It was sent from a cell phone number."

"Probably a burner," Sara said. "Whoever did this is a lying coward."

"There must be ways to figure out whose number it is, right?"

"Sure," Sara said, tapping into her phone. "We reverse-search it. I got familiar with that when I had a cheating husband. He kept taking 'work calls' out on the deck, in the cold, for hours. So I snagged his phone. That's when I found Suzanne, Regina, Karen, Kiki, and discovered what a tomcat skank he was. SwiftSearchNet is my favorite reverse-search tool. It deep-searches the entire internet, and it's faster than all the…oh…"

Sara's voice faded away and she looked at Eve, her eyes wide and startled.

Eve wouldn't have thought her insides could drop still lower than they already were, but they did. Like an express elevator. A hard, sickening plunge.

"Who?" she asked, though she already knew. "Who is it? Show me."

"Baby," Sara whispered. "I am so, so sorry." Reluctantly, she turned her phone so Eve could see the screen, and the name in the search box.

Marcus James Moss.

Eighteen

"Are you sure you don't want to call the doctor?" Marcus asked Eve again as they walked into his apartment. "She can come here. She's always on call for us."

"No," Eve said. "I don't need a doctor."

Marcus studied her face, worried. She really did not look good. Colorless and haunted. Switched off. Like a house with all the window shades drawn.

After Tilda's speech, before the dancing started, she'd told him she was feeling sick and needed to go home. She'd urged him to stay. She'd said she could take a car and go home alone.

Hell, no. If she was sick, he needed to take care of her.

"Can I go out to the pharmacy for you?" he asked. "I can get anything you need."

"No," she repeated, taking off her coat. "There's no need."

Marcus felt helpless. "I wish there was something I could do to help."

Eve unhooked the gold chain necklace that he'd given her to go with the golden dress. "I heard something very upsetting at the gala," she said.

Hairs rose on his nape. "What happened?"

"Trevor Wexford got an anonymous tip that my Corzo research was falsified."

Marcus's jaw dropped. "That's a huge lie!"

"I know," Eve said. "But someone is trying to sabotage me."

"Trevor Wexford, you said?" Marcus asked. "He's an asshole and an idiot. I'm guessing that whatever he saw won't affect the other investors."

"Wrong. They're pulling out, one after another. Henry O'Calloran, Richard Martelle, both gone. And in the car going home, I got a text from Annabelle Harlow. She's putting a hold on her investment, too. The others will follow. They're spooked."

"We'll fix it, Eve," he said. "I'll talk to them. All of them."

"Will you."

Her flat tone was so unlike her usual voice, it alarmed him. "What the hell is that supposed to mean?" he demanded.

"I'm just wondering. How do you propose to fix this dilemma? Corzo, tragically orphaned once again. What's your brilliant solution, Marcus?"

"I definitely will try to find a solution, but I don't understand your tone," he said.

"Never mind my tone. It's been a rough night, and I'm miserable. I want to know how you would solve my problem."

"First, I find out who spread the rumor," he said. "I expose him, or her. Then I talk to the investors and offer my personal guarantee as to the authenticity of your research."

"Ah," she said. "Very generous of you."

He stared at her. "The hell? Why do you sound sarcastic? What is it with you tonight?"

"No, please, go on. What will you do if they're still too scared to commit?"

"If they have any brains, they'll get over themselves and jump back on board."

"And if they don't have brains? A lot of people don't. And even smart people make poor decisions when they get scared."

Marcus shrugged. "Then we find new, smarter investors who have more nerve."

"Everyone will have heard the rumors," she said. "The project will be irreversibly tainted. Corzo will be damaged goods. No one will want to touch it."

"We'll fix it, Eve," he insisted. "We'll rebrand. Worst-case scenario, you could always count on MossTech. We could provide the funding to develop Corzo, if you don't find any other options you like better."

Her eyes fixed on him, bright and searching. "So, MossTech buying my idea and owning it? That's your solution?"

"That's 'a' solution," he said grimly. "Let me work on it, for God's sake. I just wanted you to know that there are always options."

But she wasn't listening anymore. Her eyes were bleak, faraway.

"So it's true," she whispered. "I did it again. With the pinpoint accuracy of a guided missile. Just like Walter or Hugh, or Doug. I hooked up with another guy who wants to rob me blind. I swear to God, it's like I'm under a curse."

Marcus sucked in air, horrified. "What? Are you talking about me?"

"The tip was sent from a cell phone registered to your name," she told him. "I don't recognize the number, but it's registered to you. Sara reverse-searched it."

"Let me see that number." He held out his hand.

Eve took her phone from her evening bag, opened the message and handed it to him. Marcus opened it, read the opening message.

Did you think Corzo was too good to be true? You were right. See attached.

He paged through some of the attached documents. "I've never seen this message before," he said. "I certainly did not send it."

"Do you recognize the phone number?" Eve asked.

He hesitated for a second. "Yes," he admitted. "That's a number that I used before I met you. Mostly for hookups. That phone's been missing for weeks."

"Missing," Eve said. "That's convenient. You never gave me that number."

"Of course not," he said. "That phone was for people that I didn't want to take calls from during my working day. I made a point of keeping my sex life completely separate from work and family. Until I met you."

"What became of that phone?"

"I don't know." He was feeling hunted. "It disappeared. I lost it."

"Lost it?" she repeated slowly. "Marcus. You're

the most careful, meticulous, uber-controlled person I know. You never lose things."

"I lost that phone," he repeated. "I didn't think about it much, though. I didn't need it after I met you. It barely crossed my mind. I was very occupied with you."

"I suppose I should be flattered to get the main number and not the one for the side girls and the one-offs," she said. "Quite the honor to be singled out like that."

"You believe I would do this to you? If anyone, it was Jerome. Caleb said he would come after us. But I did not see this coming."

She slipped off her heels and headed upstairs, shoes dangling from her fingertips. "It's easy and convenient to blame Jerome. He's already cast himself as the bad guy."

He followed her. "Eve, come on. I'm not a damned idiot. If I had been sabotaging you, I wouldn't have done it from a phone registered in my name!"

"Is that supposed to comfort me?" She headed for the bathroom, where she leaned over the sink and popped out her contact lenses.

He stood in the doorway as she tucked them into their cases and covered them with saline solution. "I would never steal from you," he said. "Or anyone. It's not who I am."

Eve put on her glasses, and pushed past him into the bedroom, unfastening the golden gown. She kept her back carefully turned to him as she hung up the dress. She pulled jeans, a tee and a wool sweater out of the drawer, and dressed quickly, then pulled a pair of white kicks out of his closet. She sat on the bed to pull them on.

He was starting to panic. "Eve, are you listening? Are you leaving me?"

Her eyes were so bleak, it was like a punch to the chest. "I need alone time," she said. "To figure out what is going on. I can't do that with you taking up all the air and scrambling my brain." She tied her shoes and rose, slipping her laptop into its carrying bag and hoisting it over her shoulder. "This marriage thing," she said. "It won't work if you're using me. I can't let myself be used again. I'm sorry."

"But I'm not! You're making a bad call!"

"I'm a scientist," she said. "I make decisions based on the evidence. Wherever it leads me. Regardless of how I feel, or what I might have hoped."

"Bullshit," he said. "This is a knee-jerk reaction to all the guys who screwed you over before. I didn't do that, and I never would. I swear it, Eve. Again."

"I can't stand being made a fool of for the umpteenth time," she said.

"Don't go," he pleaded. "Let's figure this out together. I'll show you it wasn't me. I don't know how yet, but I will. The truth always comes out."

She stopped in the bedroom doorway and turned. "Speaking of the truth coming out, will you tell me something, Marcus?"

"Anything," he said rashly.

"Is it true that you picked my name out of a bag? In front of your admin staff at MossTech? Like a party game. Pin the tail on the donkey. Fish the gullible geek bride out of the hat. Who's the lucky girl? Ha, ha, very jolly."

Marcus stopped breathing. "It wasn't like that," he

said. "I hadn't even met you yet. And how is this even relevant?"

"I guess it's not. It just makes me feel even more ridiculous, that's all. Eve Seaton, eternally the butt of the joke. God knows I should be used to it by now."

He followed her out the bedroom door, down the hall, down the stairs. "Eve, let me show you—"

"I've seen enough. I'm done for now. Goodbye, Marcus."

She grabbed her jacket and purse. He reached the bottom of the stairs in time to see tears streaming from her eyes as the elevator door slid shut between them.

He stood there for a long time. Minutes, hours. Eventually he forced his muscles to unlock and wandered from room to room. At one point, he found a chair near the back of his legs, so he sat, clumsily.

Jerome. This was Jerome's doing. He found his phone, and selected his uncle's number.

Jerome answered right away, as if he'd been waiting for this call.

"Marcus." His voice was cool and dragging. "At this hour? I'm an old man. I need my rest."

"You're responsible for this, aren't you?"

Jerome made a scoffing sound. "Throw me a rope, boy. What's this about?"

"Don't deny it," Marcus said. "You sent that tip to Eve's investors with my phone. The one you must have stolen. You want her to think that I'm trying to take Corzo."

"It would be a slick business move, if you had done it," Jerome observed. "I'd congratulate you for it. Corzo would be a jewel in MossTech's crown. I'd respect you far more if you'd own it, and not playact to soothe the little lady's ruffled feelings. But I understand your position. You're whipped, boy. It hurts to watch."

"I'm not playacting," he said.

"No? Is she standing there with you, listening to this conversation? Is this why you're putting on all this touching outrage? For her benefit?"

"It's just you and me," Marcus said. "She's gone."

Jerome grunted thoughtfully. "That's women for you. Flighty, changeable."

"Fuck you, Jerome."

"No need to be crude," Jerome chided. "This might be a blessing for you."

A harsh laugh jerked out of his throat. "Oh, yeah? How do you figure?"

"It's best to learn the truth about women early," Jerome said. "I learned late, and I suffered for it. It always blows up on you eventually, Marcus. You can't let yourself get attached. Keep women at a distance. Enjoy them, certainly, but keep them in their place."

"I'm not interested in love advice from you."

Jerome was undaunted. "She would've gotten tired of you, when she'd gotten what she could get out of you. You'd start looking at the other women trying to get your attention. Face it. You're a rich man. That's all women can see. They don't see you. They might pretend, but they can't pretend forever."

Marcus wanted to shout him down, prove him wrong, but his voice had frozen.

"So?" Jerome prompted. "Maybe this will be the lesson that sinks in. I got mine, years ago. It's time for you to get yours. Let her go. Better to face reality sooner rather than later."

"Yeah, and that works out great for you, doesn't it,

Uncle? You trashed my marriage to get your greedy claws into MossTech. Are you happy now?"

"I wouldn't say 'happy,'" Jerome responded. "But a man takes his victories when he can. It's the only satisfaction one ever gets in this world."

"Cold comfort," Marcus said.

"Maybe. Better cold than nothing."

"I don't want to be like you," Marcus said.

Jerome's low laugh was full of bitterness. "I don't blame you, boy."

Marcus closed the call. How ironic. That conversation, full of hostility and manipulation, was probably the most real and personal interaction he'd ever had with Jerome. Cold comfort for sure.

His phone dropped. Time crawled by. He stared out at the city, a howling ache inside him. Memories were floating up again, from that hurting inside place that he'd never wanted to feel again. Pain and fear. Grief. That endless, sinking cold ache.

He's driving me crazy. I have got to get a break. For his own safety, understand?

Safety. Huh. Like he was so safe now, with that screaming black hole inside him. Hell, maybe it would've ended like this anyway. Love ended. Mom's love certainly had.

He was done with them. Eve and her trust issues, Gran and her stupid mandate, his brother and sister, and their nudging and maneuvering. Jerome's lies and traps. MossTech. To hell with it. All of it.

But first, he'd fix this mess. He'd failed to protect Eve and Corzo from his uncle, so his first task was to save her funding. Afterward, he was out of here. Someplace warm, with a beach. A good natural climate for orchids. Flowers told no lies, nor did they believe any.

They were all that might keep him from turning into Uncle Jerome.

Nineteen

"Yes, I understand." Eve's voice cracked as she spoke. "I'll come in first thing tomorrow to pick them up. Thanks. Have a nice day."

She closed the call, laying the phone on the table. Gingerly, as if handling a loaded gun.

Sara stood there in the kitchen, the pot of steaming French-press coffee she'd been about to pour in her hand. "Who was that?" Sara asked. "What do you have to pick up?"

"The divorce papers." Her voice felt choked, so she coughed to clear it. "I have to take them to Marcus to sign."

"And will he?"

"I guess I'll find out when I call him," Eve said. "We haven't spoken in weeks."

She squeezed her hands together, fighting it until

suddenly, she couldn't anymore. Her face dissolved, and the tears slipped out. "I'm so sorry I ruined this for the team."

"Oh, honey." Sara put the coffee down and hurried over to the table, pulling a chair close so she could wrap Eve in a tight hug. "Don't feel bad about that. We knew it was a long shot. This whole thing sucks. Mostly for you."

"I'm so angry, but I miss him, too," she said. "And I miss who I was with him. The way the world felt. It feels dull and empty and stupid now."

"He's a filthy son of a bitch for doing this to you," Sara said. "You don't deserve it. You really don't, babe. You're the best person I know."

"Thanks." Eve gave her a wan smile. "Sorry I'm such a mess."

"Oh, please," Sara said, rolling her eyes. "When I called Michel to sign the divorce papers, I cried for three days. Michel was a philandering slut, but we shared some great times, and it was so hard to let go. The ninety-day waiting period was a torture of second-guessing myself." She fished out a tissue and handed it over.

Eve gratefully made use of it. "He was so convincing. He made me feel like I was a goddess come down to earth just for him. And it was so great to be with someone who actually got what I do, you know?"

"He might have 'got it' a little too well," Sara said ruefully.

Eve started to laugh, but the laughter swiftly morphed into tears.

"Oh, crap. I'm sorry," Sara said hastily. "I didn't mean to rub salt in the wound."

"I would never have dreamed he'd do that to me." She hid her face in the tissue. "He was so supportive. He busted his ass at the forum. And then he turns around and undermines all the amazing work he'd done. It was all an incredibly expensive, complicated, seductive trap. And I tumbled right into it."

"We might as well take it as a twisted compliment," Sara said in philosophical tones. "But the lying, scheming bastard has definitely got issues."

"Speaking of scheming bastards, I never dreamed that Walter would rob me, either," Eve said dolefully. "Or Hugh, for that matter. You'd think that growing up watching my dad would have vaccinated me against men like him, but it seems to have had the opposite effect. It left me with a huge blind spot. I'll never be able to trust my own instincts when it comes to men. I should swear off them completely."

"Come on, honey, don't think that way. You are not the problem here. You are enormously lovable. You deserve love."

"But it felt like Marcus loved me," Eve wailed. "It's so confusing. I don't know what to think. Red could be blue, day could be night, for all I know. Who can tell, if you can't trust your own perceptions?"

"You'll trust yourself again someday," Sara said. "But you have a couple of hard tasks ahead of you." She held up one finger. "One, call Marcus about the papers." She held up another finger. "Two, go get him to sign. It'll be awful, but you'll live."

Eve closed her eyes, rubbing them. "God," she whispered.

"Do the first one right now, before you psych yourself out of it," Sara urged. "Cross it off the list."

It was good advice. She reached for her phone and found Marcus's number. Her fingers shook. She hit Call, and it rang twice before the line opened.

"Marcus here," he said.

His voice was so flat, she barely recognized it.

"Hello, Marcus. It's Eve," she said.

"I know."

Of course he knew. His smartphone had told him. Such a stupid thing to say.

She inhaled carefully, taking her time. *Do not babble. Do not stammer. Just don't.*

"I, ah, called because I…" Her voice ran out of sound, like a printer running out of ink.

"Because?" he prompted, after a few seconds.

"I, um, I have the papers ready," she said. "The divorce papers. I'm going to get them from my lawyer tomorrow morning. I was wondering if you would… I mean, if we could…" She swallowed, and tried again, from the top. "We have to meet. To sign the papers. So I can file."

She counted six breaths before Marcus finally replied. "Of course," he said. "Let's meet in the law offices of MossTech tomorrow. Is eleven good for you?"

Like she would quibble. Like she had any kind of gainful occupation. Her life was scorched earth.

"Certainly," she said. "Eleven is fine. See you then."

"Till tomorrow. Goodbye, Eve."

Such finality in his voice. Eve closed the call and stared into space. Her chest ached.

"Is he going to contest it?" Sara asked. "Will he give you any trouble?"

"No trouble at all," she quavered. "He'll be as relieved as I am to have it over with."

Sara pried another tissue out of the pack and passed it to her. Eve pressed it to her eyes, only opening them when an odd thumping sound got her attention.

Sara was setting various items on the table. The pot of steaming coffee. Three bottles of liqueur. A big bar of fine dark chocolate. She filled their mugs more than halfway with coffee, then splashed in a generous shot of Baileys, and other things that Eve's eyes were too tear-blinded to identify. She topped it off with a slug of heavy cream.

"What's this?" Eve asked.

"Today calls for a special coffee," Sara informed her. "You're not driving, because I'm not letting you go anywhere, and you need a Dutch courage to take divorce papers to the great and powerful Marcus Moss."

Eve eyed the doctored coffee dubiously. "And meet with Marcus hungover?"

"Don't wimp out on me, girl." Flakes of chocolate drifted over the table as Sara started grating dark chocolate onto the drinks and then stirred Eve's with a cinnamon stick. She broke off a chunk of chocolate and leaned it against the mug. "I was a bartender back in grad school, remember? This was one of my most decadent creations. Go on. Try it."

Eve took a sip and had to smile. "Wow. It's delicious. And extremely strong. I bet my entire calorie count for the day is in this one mug."

"Probably," Sara agreed. She lifted her mug. "Here's to facing scary, painful obstacles. And to soldiering on in the face of crushing disappointment."

Eve raised her mug. "To soldiering on," she repeated. "And to loyal friends that you can cry on."

That melted them down, and they hugged tightly.

By the time they got back to the coffee, it was stone-cold, but whatever.

They just had to make the best of it.

Marcus laid his cell phone on the greenhouse table and returned to pruning the hibiscus. Maddie and Tilda and Annika stood there, watching him as if he were a bomb that could explode at any moment.

"Who was that?" Maddie asked.

He braced himself. "Eve," he said.

After a few moments, Maddie and Tilda exchanged exasperated glances.

"And?" Maddie prompted. "What did she want?"

"The divorce papers are ready to sign. Tomorrow morning."

Maddie gulped. Tilda turned away, her slim shoulders sagging.

"Look, I'm sorry," he said. "I tried. But if I'd known how hard I was going to crash, I would've bailed a long time ago."

"But it's not your fault," Annika said earnestly. "Mommy said that you didn't even do the bad thing Eve thought you did. So why don't you try to explain?"

Marcus controlled his frustration, which was inappropriate to express to a nine-year-old. "I tried that, honey. But she's been burned before, so she won't listen to me."

"But it's stupid!" Annika said rebelliously. "And it's not fair! She's really great, and I really liked her. And she should stay with you!"

"A lot of things in life aren't fair," he said. "We just have to deal with it. Hey, you know what? I think Jocelyn might have left some of those ice cream bars that you like in the freezer. Why don't you see if you can find one. She puts them in the bottom drawer."

Annika's face lit up. "Yum," she said. "Do you guys want one, too?"

"Thanks, not for me, baby," he told her.

Tilda and Maddie also declined, and Annika scampered off into the apartment in search of her ice cream.

Marcus turned to glower at his sister and his sister-in-law. "You two brought Annika here as a human shield, right? That's a dirty trick."

"Depends on how you look at it," Maddie said. "There's only so rude, sulky and self-involved you can be when your innocent and adoring little niece is in earshot. It seems logical to me to use her to bring out your best self."

That jerked a dry laugh from his throat. "Best self, my ass."

"You're going to sign those papers with no complaint?" Tilda said, her voice hushed but impassioned. "That woman loves you, Marcus!"

"I can't take this roller coaster," he told her. "Can I persuade her, can I prove myself to her, can I convince her? So far, the answer is no. She won't take my calls."

"So you're giving up," Tilda said.

"I'm cutting my losses, Til," Marcus said. "I've already lost my job, and my mind, and my career, as I know it. So all of you, for God's sake, back off."

Maddie's face was tight. "I'm so sorry, Marcus. I know you got in really deep with Eve. Can't you try one last time to get through to her?"

"Not without setting myself up to get freshly destroyed. Please stop asking."

Maddie's face crumpled. "It's so stupid! Damn Jerome for wrecking this for you. I thought you'd finally broken through. That maybe you could even be…"

"Be what?" Marcus demanded.

Maddie threw up her hands. "Happy," she said angrily. "It was a long shot, I know. You're uptight, defensive. Always have been, since we were little. But you weren't with Eve. All of a sudden, it seemed like happiness might not be too much to ask for you anymore."

"I thought so, too," he said. "Joke's on us, huh?"

"Don't," Maddie burst out. "Just don't! I hate when you're like this. Brittle and cold. Shutting me out, shutting everyone out. I hate it!"

"Stop hounding me," he snarled. "I can't deal with you on top of the rest of it."

"The rest of what?" asked Annika's bright, piping voice as she skipped back in with her ice cream bar, nibbling on the white chocolate tip.

"Nothing," Marcus muttered.

"You should have some ice cream, too, Uncle Marcus," Annika said, studying his face. "You're thinner, and you've got smudges under your eyes, like Daddy did when he had the flu. Do you have the flu?"

"No, honey," he said wearily. "I'm just tired. Don't worry about me."

Annika grabbed his waist, squeezing him tightly. The hug made something in his chest soften. It hurt. Annika was a sweet little girl. He hugged her back.

"Your new flower is really pretty," she offered.

It was true. The stubborn hibiscus had finally bloomed. Its velvety petals faded from a very pale yellow to salmon to lavender to deep, cobalt blue on the frilly tip. It was spectacular, but he wasn't capable of enjoying it. He saw the world in shades of gray. "It's the first time this one ever bloomed," he told her.

"What's it called?" Annika asked.

"It doesn't have a name yet," he told her. "It's the first one that's ever existed."

"Cool." Annika eyes turned crafty. "You should bring Eve some flowers. Girls like flowers."

"Honey, please. Don't bother him. We talked about this, remember?"

"It's okay." Marcus ruffled her hair. "It's a good idea, but the timing might be off."

"Let's go, baby," Tilda said to her little girl.

Marcus suffered through a series of strangling hugs from all three of the Moss females before he was blessedly alone again. Just the soothing company of his flowers, which did not scold or admonish him. They just existed, glowing with beauty and color, being their generous and radiant selves with no apparent effort.

As he stared at the blossoms, it occurred to him that Annika's naive advice could be the seed of something useful. Flowers were something he and Eve understood instinctively. She wouldn't be on guard against the silent language of flowers.

Of course, he might also end up looking stupid, obvious and blatantly manipulative, but what the hell. She already thought the worst of him. He had nothing left to lose. No matter how she took it, offering her the newly blooming hibiscus would be a classy final gesture.

But he needed to pack his stuff. Have his bags in his car, and a plane ticket and passport in his pocket. From the lawyer's office straight to the airport. It was in everyone's best interests that he put distance between himself and the rest of humanity.

Signing those papers would take all the self-control and class that he had left.

Twenty

Eve stared across the courtyard of the MossTech complex, focusing on the water that ran smoothly over the huge granite globe in the center. Her eyes stung.

Beyond it, next to the lab building, was the soaring, thirty-story Kobe Tower, which housed the legal department of MossTech. It was a handsome building, but today, it loomed over her with a menacing air.

She'd never been so miserable, and it was no surprise, after overindulging in Sara's decadent coffee drinks yesterday. After crashing at Sara's, her friend had rousted her out of bed this morning, revved her up with black coffee and Excedrin, and shoved her out the door to go collect the papers from the divorce lawyer.

She felt a rush of gratitude for Sara, who had stuck by her through all the tears. Starting back with Walter's betrayal. Intensifying exponentially with Marcus's. Sara had offered to accompany her, but Eve had decided that this was a job for herself alone, rigorously dressed in her big-girl panties. Besides, Sara was a spitfire. After Michel, she was angry at men in general, and right now, at Marcus in particular, and Eve wanted to keep things cool and polite today. She'd slide in and out with her signed documents, and move on with whatever the rest of her life would be.

It looked hard and bleak and boring.

"Eve? Eve Seaton?" blared a husky female voice behind her.

Eve spun, heart pounding. "Who?"

"Oh, relax! It's just me! Sorry I startled you." It was Annabelle Harlow, one of the previous Corzo investors.

"Hello, Ms. Harlow," she said, with stiff courtesy. "Good to see you again."

"Oh, hell, call me Annabelle. I wasn't even sure it was you. You're so pale. You've lost weight. Have you been sick, honey?"

Eve smiled politely. True, she didn't look her best. Eating had been a challenge, and she was hungover as hell. She'd tried to salvage the situation with makeup, but clearly her efforts had fallen short of the mark.

"I'm fine," she said. "How are you?"

"Great, now that I heard the news!" The older woman's hearty clap on her back made Eve lurch forward with a cough. "I'm glad I caught you! I was just in a meeting with Caleb and Tilda, discussing partnership possibilities for her FarEye project, and kaboom, I run into you! It's fortuitous. I was meaning to arrange a meeting as soon as possible."

"Fortuitous?" Eve was bewildered. "Didn't you decide to step back from Corzo?"

Annabelle looked blank. "Haven't you been talking to Marcus?"

"Ah...not about that, no," she admitted. "Not lately. I haven't seen him for a while. Last I heard, the investors had pulled out. That was where I left it."

Annabelle blinked. "Young lady, you have some communication issues with your husband!"

Hah. Wasn't that the understatement of the freaking century. "Busy lives," she said, forcing a smile. "You know how it is. Clue me in. What did you want to meet about?"

"To get back into the project, of course!" Annabelle said heartily. "After the Cold Creek Retreat, there's simply no question about it."

"Cold Creek Retreat? What's that?"

Annabelle's jaw dropped. "Sweetheart, you don't know a damn thing about what's been happening lately?"

"Annabelle, just give it to me straight, with no theatrics, please." Despite her best efforts, her tone was getting sharp.

"Now don't get all agitated," Annabelle soothed. "First Marcus called us together, and bought us a spectacular dinner at Canlis, where he proceeded to tell us the tale."

"What tale?"

Annabelle waved an expressive hand. "The marriage mandate, the bonkers uncle, the stolen phone. Such a story! I don't know what was more fabulous, the food or the entertainment. That man is easy on the eyes, eh? And the duck with pumpkin, the oyster emulsion, oh, my Lord! And their apple cake is to die for—"

"Annabelle. Get to the point."

"Sorry. So anyhow, he offered to pay for an audit team of our own choosing to go through the Corzo research material with a fine-tooth comb and judge the veracity of that malicious rumor. So we took him up on it. What the hell, right? It was his dime, and we got to choose our own impartial experts. So the experts did their thing, and then last weekend he had us out for a retreat at the Cold Creek Lodge. For two days, he wined us and dined us while the panel presented its findings. The upshot was, Corzo is truly groundbreaking. An unbelievable opportunity. We were all convinced, except for the Wexfords. They backed out because Callista didn't want drama. My ass, hmm? That snotty little minx lives for drama. But frankly, Corzo is better off without them."

Eve gazed at her, blank and speechless "I... I... That's incredible."

Annabelle patted her shoulder. "We're sorry we ever doubted you. And oh, that Marcus." Annabelle wriggled her shoulders in appreciation. "He believes in your project so passionately. You would've thought Corzo was his own baby, the way he fought for it. Give that fellow a pat on the head, if you know what I mean. It's good to reward them, when they deserve it, eh?" Annabelle tossed her head back with a bawdy laugh.

"Thanks so much, Annabelle," Eve said. "I'm very excited to meet with you. As soon as possible. My team will be so thrilled."

"I'm tickled to death that I got to be the bearer of good news!" Annabelle bubbled. "Such a privilege!"

"Um, yes," Eve stammered. "But please, you'll have to excuse me right now. I'm late for a meeting. But we'll talk again. Very soon."

"Yes, of course we will. Good luck, whatever your meeting's about!"

Eve hurried across the courtyard and into the tower lobby. She took the elevator and walked into the legal department, five minutes late. The lobby was huge and bright and spacious, extremely minimalist and luxe, like all the MossTech buildings.

The elegant woman at the reception desk spotted her and murmured into her phone. Soon afterward, another equally elegant woman appeared to lead her to her destination. The woman's perfectly made-up face made Eve glance around for a reflective surface, just to see how red and puffy her eyes were, and if she had frizz in front of her ears. She stopped herself, with some effort. That way lay madness.

The girl stopped outside a conference room. "Mr. Moss is waiting for you," she said. "And Mr. Cogswell should be along in a few minutes." She opened the door. "Mr. Moss, Ms. Seaton is here," she announced.

Marcus stood with his back to her, looking out the window. He wore an elegant dark gray suit.

He turned. Her breath caught. After a few weeks of not seeing him, the force of his beauty just hit her all over again, with raw force. But he was thinner. There were lines in his face, shadowed eyes, and his mouth looked flat.

"Hello, Marcus," she said.

"Hello, Eve," he replied.

She walked into the room. There was a flowering plant on the table. It was large and lush, and its spectacular flowers were on full display.

She forced herself to break the silence. "I ran into

Annabelle Harlow outside. She said she wanted back into the Corzo project."

His eyebrows rose. "Good news," he said. "And? So?"

"Don't play dumb," she said. "Explain this. She told me about a luxury meal at Canlis where you revealed all your private family drama to the investors. An independent audit of my research for them, which you paid for yourself. A luxury retreat at Cold Creek Lodge while the panel walked them through the results. All at your expense, and not a word to me. What the hell?"

"Why should I have said anything? You wouldn't answer my calls. It seemed undignified and creepy to keep bugging you. Besides, I figured you'd hear about it from the investors themselves. I'm surprised it didn't happen sooner."

"Annabelle was shocked that I didn't know."

His mouth twitched. "Annabelle gets off on being shocked."

"Yeah, I guess," she said faintly. "So, um. Thank you. For doing that."

"No need. I couldn't confirm it, but I'm sure that it was my uncle who tried to kill the project. So I considered it my responsibility to clean up the mess. Everything's in place except for the Wexfords and we don't want them anyway. I'm investing my own money to cover the shortfall. My personal funds, to be clear. Not MossTech. I'm not associated with them anymore."

She was startled. "You're not?"

He shrugged. "No. Once I'm divorced, control of the company goes to Jerome anyway."

"Right," she said faintly. "Of course."

"It's good timing, calling when you did. I'm leaving

the country, and we needed to take care of this before I go."

That hit her like a punch, deep inside. "Going where?"

"Indonesia. I'll probably settle there. I'll sell the apartment. I'm leaving this afternoon."

She felt light-headed. "This afternoon," she repeated, inanely. "You're not going to...try again? To find someone to marry?"

A brief smile came and went on his face. "No. It's over."

"Oh, God," she whispered.

"We'll be fine without MossTech," he said. "We'll do other useful things with our time. Don't sweat it."

"It's a shame, to let that maniac have MossTech."

"I couldn't agree more, but what can you do," he said. "Sorry to rush you, but I have a plane to catch, so can we get on with this? I'll sign the papers and get out of your hair, and Cogswell can explain the terms of my Corzo investment to you after I leave."

She moved like a puppet. Clumsy gestures. Opening her briefcase. Pulling out the documents. Marcus leaned across the table and twitched the papers toward himself.

"They're flagged," she said faintly. "With, ah, stickers. The places you need to sign. I brought a copy of the prenup for reference, though I'm sure your lawyer has yours. Do you need to have your lawyer review the papers?"

He leafed swiftly through the documents from beginning to end. "No need," he said. "This looks like it's all in order." He leaned over, a pen in his hand.

"Stop." Eve's voice came out louder than she'd intended.

He froze, looking up. "What?"

"Things are changing faster than I have time to catch up," she said. "I'm confused."

"I'm not," he said flatly. "My position has never changed. I told you the truth then, and I'm telling it now. All I've been doing lately is trying to make it right for you."

"But things are different now," she said. "If you kept your side of the bargain, I should keep mine, too."

He looked away for a moment, and briefly shook his head. "I'm glad you're convinced now," he said. "But I wish you'd had more faith in me before."

"Me, too," she said. "I was reactive, and stupid. And I'm sorry. Like you said, I was making decisions emotionally, because of past baggage. All I can do now is try to make it right for you."

He looked up, his eyes keen. "Make it right how?"

She drew in a shaky, nervous breath. "Um. Well. We could go back to our original agreement, and stay officially married. If you want to maintain control of MossTech. And if you, um, still want to be married to me. After everything that's happened. I'd totally understand if you didn't."

She held her breath. She'd rolled the dice. All or nothing.

"No," Marcus said harshly.

Eve kept her face blank. So it was nothing, then.

Okay. Dignity. Dignity was key.

"I understand," she whispered. "It's all right."

"What I mean is, I'm not doing this half-assed. I won't stay married to you unless it's completely for real, and we figure out how to trust each other. One hundred percent. Forever. Till death do us part."

It took a while before his words would penetrate. "You mean…" Her voice faded.

"I want you," he said. "The whole deal. Like we had before, but bigger, deeper, stronger. So strong, nobody could ever push us apart with lies again."

"I'm so sorry about that," she said. "I was wired to expect betrayal."

"So we'll rewire," he said. "I love you, Eve, and there will be no betrayal from me, ever. Please, believe that."

Joy started to glow in her chest. Soft and bright, like the sun emerging from a cloud. "Yes," she whispered, her voice choked. "Oh, my God, yes."

With tear-blurred eyes, she couldn't tell if he ran around the table or leaped across it, but suddenly they were in each other's arms, locked in a desperate, pleading kiss. Trying to make up for the misery and mistakes of the past weeks.

The door clicked open. They heard a gasp, and an embarrassed chuckle. "Sorry," a man's voice murmured. "I take it we're, ah, postponing the appointment?"

"Get lost, Leonard," Marcus rasped.

"Sure thing." Leonard yanked the door shut, laughing.

Marcus reached out to engage the door lock, and then he hoisted her onto the conference room table. The potted plant rattled perilously, almost toppling when their weight hit the table. Marcus reached out to steady it and pushed it out of harm's way.

"I don't remember that blossom." Her voice was choked with emotion. "Is that the hibiscus you showed me? The one that was holding out on you?"

"Yes. It finally bloomed. Annika suggested I bring it to you. She told me girls like flowers, and I thought, hell, yeah. No girl likes flowers like Eve Seaton likes flowers."

"You thought right," she told him. "It's spectacular. What's it called?"

Marcus was smiling helplessly, his fingers wound into her hair, stroking it like he couldn't believe she was there. "I named it 'Eve's Kiss.'"

Anything she might have said in reply was lost against his hungry mouth, but that was no problem at all.

They understood each other perfectly.

* * * * *

Don't miss a single book
in New York Times *bestselling author*
Shannon McKenna's
Dynasties: Tech Tycoons series!

Their Marriage Bargain
The Marriage Mandate
How to Marry a Bad Boy
Married by Midnight

Exclusively available from
Harlequin Desire.

WE HOPE YOU ENJOYED
THIS BOOK FROM
HARLEQUIN
DESIRE

*Luxury, scandal, desire—welcome to
the lives of the American elite.*

Be transported to the worlds of oil barons, family dynasties,
moguls and celebrities. Get ready for juicy plot twists,
delicious sensuality and intriguing scandal.

6 NEW BOOKS AVAILABLE EVERY MONTH!

#2905 THE OUTLAW'S CLAIM

Westmoreland Legacy: The Outlaws • by Brenda Jackson

Rancher Maverick Outlaw and Sapphire Bordella are friends with occasional benefits. But when Phire must marry at her father's urging, their relationship ends...until they learn she's carrying Maverick's baby. Now he'll stop at nothing to stake his claim...

#2906 CINDERELLA MASQUERADE

Texas Cattleman's Club: Ranchers and Rivals • by LaQuette

Ready to break out of her shell, Dr. Zanai James agrees to go all out for the town's masquerade ball and meets handsome rancher Jayden Lattimore. Their attraction is instantaneous, but can their connection survive meddling families bent on keeping them apart?

#2907 MARRIED BY MIDNIGHT

Dynasties: Tech Tycoons • by Shannon McKenna

Ronnie Moss is in trouble. The brilliant television host needs a last-minute husband to fulfill her family's marriage mandate before she turns thirty—at midnight. Then comes sexy stranger Wes Brody, who volunteers himself. But is this convenient arrangement too good to be true?

#2908 SNOWED IN SECRETS

Angel's Share • by Jules Bennett

After distillery owner Sara Hawthorne and Ian Ford spend one hot night together, they don't expect to see each other again...until he shows up for their scheduled interview about her family business. Now snowed in, can they keep it professional?

#2909 WHAT HAPPENS AFTER HOURS

404 Sound • by Kianna Alexander

Recording studio exec Miles Woodson needs a showstopping act for his charity talent show, and R & B superstar Cambria Harding fits the bill. But when long days working together become steamy nights, can these opposites make both their passion project and relationship work?

#2910 BAD BOY WITH BENEFITS

The Kane Heirs • by Cynthia St. Aubin

Sent to audit his distillery, Marlowe Kane should keep her distance from bad boy owner Law Renaud. But when a storm prevents her from getting home, they can't resist, and their relationship awakens a passion in both that could cost them everything...

*Returning to her hometown, brokenhearted journalist
Adaline Harlow is supposed to write an exposé on
Colter Ward, Texas's Sexiest Bachelor, and that
assignment does not include falling for him! As the
attraction grows, will they break their no-love-allowed
rule for a second chance at happiness?*

Read on for a sneak peek at
Most Eligible Cowboy
by USA TODAY *bestselling author Stacey Kennedy.*

"You want your story. I want these women off my back…
Stay in town and agree to being my girlfriend until this
story dies down and I'll give you the exclusive you want."

"Her eyes widened. "You're serious?"

"Deadly serious," he confirmed. "I want my life back.
You need a promotion. This is a win-win for both of us."

She gave a cute wiggle on her stool. "I think you're
giving me far too much credit. Why would women care if
I'm your girlfriend?"

"I don't think you're giving yourself enough credit."
He stared at her parted lips, shining eyes, her slowly

HDEXP0922

building smile, and closed the distance between them, waiting for her to back away. When she didn't and even leaned in closer, he said, "Trust me, they'd care." He captured her mouth, cupping her warm face, telling himself the whole damn time this was a terrible idea.

Don't miss what happens next in...
Most Eligible Cowboy
by USA TODAY *bestselling author Stacey Kennedy.*

Available November 2022 wherever
Harlequin Desire books and ebooks are sold.

Harlequin.com

HDEXP0922

Love Harlequin romance?

DISCOVER.

Be the first to find out about promotions, news and exclusive content!

f Facebook.com/HarlequinBooks

y Twitter.com/HarlequinBooks

O Instagram.com/HarlequinBooks

p Pinterest.com/HarlequinBooks

You Tube YouTube.com/HarlequinBooks

ReaderService.com

EXPLORE.

Sign up for the Harlequin e-newsletter and download a free book from any series at **TryHarlequin.com**

CONNECT.

Join our Harlequin community to share your thoughts and connect with other romance readers! **Facebook.com/groups/HarlequinConnection**

HSOCIAL2021

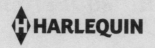

HARLEQUIN

Heartfelt or thrilling, passionate or uplifting—Harlequin is more than just happily-ever-after.

With twelve different series to choose from and new books available every month, you are sure to find stories that will move you, uplift you, inspire and delight you.

SIGN UP FOR THE HARLEQUIN NEWSLETTER

Be the first to hear about great new reads and exciting offers!

Harlequin.com/newsletters